FALLEN

A FOUR CROWNS PREQUEL

ERIN LARK MAPLES

LODESTAR LITERARY

To Katherine,
you're on the hook.

ONE

JOAQUIN

From the rooftop, I watch the huddled and bundled bustle through the square, oblivious.

Poor bastards.

Their fingers blue, noses pink, several stuff hands deep into armpits, wrap scarves up to their cheeks. The majority, though? Their faces remain transfixed by glowing screens clutched in gloved hands. They are the easiest to fool. The vulnerable. They wander our ersatz hamlet attached to a tiny rectangle, as the realities of a supernatural world flow around them.

It's too easy, sometimes. Many of us consider losing the charmstones, the glamour, and all manner of costumery. Would humans even notice?

I suppose I, too, remain tied to humanity in a twisted turn of fate. Yet with each season, that thread wears thinner until the past erodes what's left of my dark, neglected heart.

Enough self-obsessed whining. There are upsides to being reckless, pariahed. Dangerous.

For one, this combat jacket. It's a treasure, one I lifted from the trash pile of a bruiser I found choking this girl in his truck cab as he forced his way with her in a rest stop parking lot. Curious how fast a neck snaps under a little pressure—and teeth.

Anyway, my jacket is for looks, a token. Fits like a glove, too—both the shoulders and the reminder of my first kill. Have to get the sleeves sewn back on now and again, mend some rips. But you do that for the favorites in your closet.

This thing is a memento, too, of the life I never got. The one I'd never get. Army doctors would have turned this body over to science in a heartbeat, erasing my existence. Would have been easy—it's not like I had anyone left to notice my absence back then.

There I go, sad-sacking again.

I bought military boots to match my jacket. Abuela taught me never to wear other people's shoes—it's bad for your feet. I topped these steel-toed beauties off with the tightest jeans I could stand to keep me contained and decent. This body, in any form, radiates enough heat and then some. Suffice it to say, I don't get cold.

It's a good thing, as the high desert makes a brutal winter mistress. Deceptive sunshine by day, no cloud cover to retain vestiges of heat by night. Like a jilted lover, when the cold settles here for the season, she's committed.

I don't remember what it's like, being cold. Yet tonight I rub my hands together and breathe on them in a nostalgic practice as I watch those below me do the same. I can almost recall what it's like to have Lady Winter's fingers wrapped around my heart, slowing its incessant pump. Almost.

Prescott is no Las Vegas. We aren't known for strippers, race cars, or gambling. We do, however, have a historical street with quite the checkered past. Whiskey Row is notorious for liquor and deeds. Countless people stumble down the sidewalks after a night barhopping.

Not that libations are limited to one side of Courthouse Square. Across Gurley, a group of men stumble out the door of the latest eyesore of a brewery. The interior screams late-twenties testosterone. Screens on every wall, rotating wait-staff who can barely stand showing up, and enough fried food to clog an artery.

What I wouldn't give to eat like that again.

The pack hits the frigid air and retreats, pausing under the awning to shrug into coats and consult their phones. The loudest—you know his type—insists on taking the party to the next stop. Some check in with wives or girlfriends via their digital leashes, contemplating the full-on hangover they know is coming tomorrow morning. Others swipe left or right on the screen, in hopes of a local late night score. They're all the same.

In contrast, those without choices huddle in the shadows. They spent the holidays forgotten, forsaken, nestled into the corners of the courthouse, a bastion of organized oppression in the middle of the square. They occupy doorways and vestibules with what scraps of clothing they find in the ever-shifting city. Many fall prey to this brutal and punishing season.

A couple passes beneath me. One of the forsaken reaches out to pet their dog. The man holding the leash reaches in his pocket to extract a few bills. His partner jerks his coat sleeve, ushers him along.

Lights wink out in the windows of historical buildings surrounding the square. Cars creep along Montezuma, hitting every light on their way to the urban sprawl of the valley beyond.

This is Prescott. A city with more identities than history can count.

More creatures like me than any resident could guess.

And they haven't a clue, these humans.

I watch as the woman who owns the corner candle shop backs out of the front door, a bag slung over one shoulder. She presses numbers into a keypad to lock the door, then wraps a scarf around her neck. Her head twists, dark hair shining under the streetlights as she looks up and down the street before stepping onto the sidewalk. She keeps a quick clip; purple tights peeking out below a long, woolen jacket that draws my eyes to the curves she's no doubt rocking below. Probably going to the apartment of some bulked up boyfriend who loves the sight of his handprints on her cheeks. I allow

3

myself to picture her, lying on her stomach across the sheets, that raven hair splayed across the satin.

Get a grip, Joaquin.

I adjust my jeans and look away, flooding my mind with red on white, skin on grass, smoke and shouting, then deathly quiet. My urges abate, overwhelmed with rage. I harbor energy that while powerful, is slow burning with finality. Time is my only enemy.

Next to me, a scattering of pigeons peck and dawdle as though we are flighted kin here on the roof. I wave my hand in their direction, and they scatter, distrusting. They'll settle in the eaves, nesting close to stay warm until dawn.

No one else sees me up here. They never notice a dark figure leaning over the brick edge of this three-story building on Whiskey Row. I've learned to blend in with the dark, becoming one with the shadows.

I turn my attention to the sidewalk below. The bar above which I sit is a busy place. Customers push in and out of its doors long into the night. Most will leave, their bellies full and pink in their cheeks, though not all. This place is the final stop for at least one soul tonight. Might even be a peaceful end—if they allow it. Makes my job all the easier and keeps the management happy.

You see, Sharon prefers they arrive intact. She doesn't want to meet them missing a limb, burned on half their body, or otherwise disfigured. But hey, it's not like they don't have a choice in the matter.

A new figure catches my eye across the square. Just in time.

From my perch, the trees, stripped of their leaves, do little to hide the plaza. At the base of a massive oak, my target stops. He runs both hands through his hair as though considering options he knows do not exist. He walks with a hitch in his step, a confirmation I've got my guy.

He stops across the street from the bar to read the sign, one I've read myself countless times. Morgan's Publican. Boss tells me the original owners immigrated here and set up the place to match the one they left behind in the Highlands. They couldn't have known, then, what this place would become. Then again, I wonder if old Ma and Pa Morgan knew more than we think.

As I watch, my mark hesitates. He scans the sidewalk. From here, I smell the cortisol in his blood. He reads the sign once more, glances around, then slips off to the west.

He had a choice. We could've done this the easy way.

A parkour natural, I launch myself from the fire escape onto the rooftop of the building next door. With a practiced slide, I meet the edge. The only sound is the tinkle of ice hitting the sidewalk. Silent footfalls benefit my line of work. It's a decent enough job, all said and done. Wake up, get an assignment, hang out with a few buddies while you wait for your shift to start, then escort the target to their destiny. Three squares a day, a warm bed, and there isn't a much better way to await an early expiration date.

Over the side of the building, down another fire escape, and through the alley. All senses up, and let me tell you, this guy reeks. Fear has a scent, and layered within arrogance, it isn't hard to anticipate poor choices.

On the street, he takes a fast corner. I shrink into a doorway as he plows into a woman who stumbled from our neighboring bar. Whiskey Row isn't light on drinking establishments—it's part of the draw.

"Excuse me," she says, clinging to his jacket and breathing heavily into his face. She slurs her words while she pats at his chest. "I didn't see you there. Now I do."

The guy whips his head around, on high alert. Even with nothing left to lose, his kind panic at the thought of exposure.

The woman continues her sloppy seduction. "Hey, you're really cute. Maybe you could walk me home. It's not like that asshole Ray is going to do it." Her eyes go dark with momentary sobriety. "He's never walking me home again, is he?"

My mark alternates his gaze from this woman who is all but volunteering to take him into her bed and the bar where his fate awaits.

A smile stretches across the woman's face again as she

taps his chest. "You wouldn't do that to me, would you? You're one of the good ones, I can tell."

There's a moment where he takes in the tight dress, the low neckline, her candy lips. He pastes on a smile to match hers.

I read that expression a mile away—it's not like I don't have the same thought. A gorgeous woman is a universal truth. I tamp that thought down, will my urges into submission. That beast has long been caged, the key thrown away at a graveside strewn with roses and broken dreams.

This guy checks the street once before hurrying the woman down the sidewalk, his arm over her shoulder. Rushed, she steps one shoe into the crack of the sidewalk. The heel snaps off and she hobbles to keep up with him. A few more feet and she stumbles to one knee, laughing. He clutches at her, committed to his prize yet anxious about discovery.

I'm patient, focused. It would take more than some drunken acquaintance to alter his destiny.

As they stumble-walk along, she talks at him, but he says nothing, watching the shadows. She comes to an abrupt stop in front of a long-shuttered breakfast place. "Oh, look, a puppy." The dog whimpers, and she bends to stroke its ears.

He grumbles at her delay. "You shouldn't touch strange animals," he says, aware of an irony she does not know. "What if it has diseases?"

She removes her jacket to put it on the dog, warm from the alcohol coursing through her veins. "Help me carry him. I'll keep him warm at my place tonight. I can take him to the shelter in the morning."

The promise of her bed a prime motivator, the man stoops, as though to shoulder the burden of this random canine.

I am nothing if not an opportunist. Crouched, he is vulnerable.

I strike with every weapon I've got.

He screams, then bursts into flames.

I leap back, stunned, hair singed in a few tender places.

The woman shrieks and runs, the broken shoe flying off

into the night. In the morning while staving off a thundering headache, she'll tell her roommates there was a dog. An attack. They won't believe her. Chalk up the imagery to too many drinks, a broken heart, and mangled pride. Flip through the photos on her phone and find nothing.

This is convenient for me. Tracking down the one-heeled woman might take more time than you think—and I've got a busy day ahead of me.

Hands on hips, I watch the flames burn the body to dust. Ashes dissipate into the air. I shake myself off—a realignment—flex my wrists and stretch as the last bits of my assignment disappear into the air. I don't know how guys play football into their forties. Even I don't bounce back like I did when I was twenty.

On the sidewalk in the center of a dark spot left by the fire, I find a worn leather-wrapped book. I pick it up and flip it over. Instead of a Celtic knot, an acorn, or some other symbol of the Gentry, I find a four-pointed star.

I'm going to need a drink.

TWO

JOAQUIN

"Don't tell me you're on one of those fancy new year diets."

The cherry the woman insisted on adding to my bourbon lays discarded on the cocktail napkin. I peer into the glass in my hand. Golden liquid reflects my features back up to me. Shaggy hair in need of a cut, bushy brows, and so many damn eyelashes. I used to pluck them out in clumps to make my sisters squeal in feigned horror.

I meet the curious eyes of the new server. Social Distortion shirt, minimal makeup, her curls swept back in a clip. What will she do if I reach up and free those curls, wipe off some of the coal that distracts from those wide brown eyes. Bite those lips to pink them up.

Behind the bar, she reaches for a bottle on a high shelf. My gaze traces her curves wrapped up in a pair of snowflake-dotted leggings ending in faux sheepskin booties. I'd bet good money her feet were sweaty, running around in those things for a full shift. Would her toenails match the coppery pink at her fingertips?

Bottle retrieved, she leans over the bar, one eyebrow cocked. I smell coffee, a breath mint, and the remnants of a cheeseburger. Vanilla shampoo mixed with sweat fills my nostrils, and they flare in response.

8

Think of the past.

There are the pictures never far below my conscious mind. Long, chestnut hair trailing from a car window. The barrel of a Luger pointed my way, dark sunglasses shielding its owner. Guests lying strewn about the grass like giant dolls, abandoned by their owner. Late afternoon sunlight glinting off the chrome bumper as it sped away.

Ansel's latest hire looks like she either wants to shake me or take me home with her. Maybe both.

"What was that?"

"I asked if you were going to be all right. Looks like it's been a while since you had a real meal. I've got some things in my fridge…" She trails off to wait for my response.

A sheen of sweat appears above her lip as she waits. I squeeze my eyes, willing the bourbon to shut up so I can talk. I know how this would go. I know what this can cost.

"Your boss in, greenhorn?"

Hurt registers on her face. She brushes it off like a gnat in her salad. She busies herself removing glasses from the abandoned seat next to mine. "He's upstairs," she says. "But he isn't in the best of moods."

"Aw, Santa didn't bring him any presents?" I've been gone too long. My last job took a few more weeks and twice the energy I'd planned. I should know better than to leave my buddy alone this close to the anniversary, but I've got bills to pay, vengeance to fund.

"You know him," she says, a dismissal.

I down the rest of my drink, set it on the cocktail napkin stamped with the pub's logo, and head for the back stairs.

Morgan's has commanded a prominent spot on Whiskey Row since the town's inception. The multistory, brick building rents its lower level out to an art gallery. The bar and its kitchens occupy the second floor while Ansel's office, storage, and makeshift apartment are on the top floor. He lets me crash there when I'm in town.

With loads of vintage detailing and a second floor balcony from which revelers enjoy singing their debauchery to the crowds, the place is packed with charm. Inside is floor-to-ceiling walnut, the finest to be found in the early 20th century. The original structure was rougher cut but burned down in 1900. The rebuild brought a sense of class and occupation to the center of the block.

In the short hallway past the bathrooms to the stairs are a row of photographs anchored behind thin, black frames. First, the original owners, lovebirds from Inverness, stand in front of the original building with a giant key. In another, the woman holds a baby in her arms, and in the next snuggles a second baby while a young boy peeks out from behind the legs of the man. Several more frames hold collages filled with patrons raising glasses from around the hand-carved bar top in the new building.

Time marches by in the pictures. In the most recent, the great-great-granddaughter of the first owners stands behind the bar in a hand-sewn apron. She wipes at the bar top, a broad grin across her face, as the five-year-old version of my best buddy sits in a stool, clutching a sippy cup. He was a big kid back then, and now...

I can still see the child in the brooding man before me. Long, thick, sandy hair and cheery blue eyes that made for an adorable little boy are still there. But there is nothing small about the man engulfing the office chair in which he sits. He'd grown and kept growing until there aren't many who are bigger. The last photograph in the hallway is of the current bar owner and my best friend. He stoops to wrap an arm around the shoulder of a tiny older woman wearing the same apron she'd sewn for the older picture.

Ansel was the fifth generation Morgan to own the place. Blood relation was never part of his ascension.

"I come bearing news," I tease. "Would've waited downstairs but my fans wouldn't leave me alone."

I've been after Ansel for years to put up some pictures in his office. He maintains that business requires little in the way of decoration. On the wall across from his desk, he tacked a large paper calendar, the kind where you write your dentist appointments, your aunt's birthday, and a due date for the water bill. His has only a giant red circle around one date, a string of Xs marching toward it. On the desktop sits a mug that says, "Kiss me, I'm Scottish" and a handful of Morgan's Publican pens. Monitors crowd the rest of the space, one for the laptop, the other dedicated to security cameras. A wall holds a single window out to the atrium, locked.

In the corner, Ansel's dog Failinis lounges on a too-small bed. The beast is a massive wolfhound-type, long-legged and covered in a wiry, shaggy coat that never gets wet. He moans and twitches a paw in his sleep, no doubt chasing a fox through a Scottish greenscape. Ansel said the first of his line came over on the boat with his owners, sire to the generations that would follow.

I flip the latch in the window casing and crank the glass open. I peer out into the dark space. Nothing stirs between the buildings, save the crumpled advertisement and a gray cat stalking some unseen prey. A bitter breeze whistles in from the rooftops, and I shiver.

"You're almost there," I say into the night, not meeting Ansel's eyes. "So close." Three rotations and the window snugs closed.

Ansel reaches for his mug, gives it a swirl, and sniffs. "Twenty-three. Twenty-three-godsdamn-days." He takes a sip, then makes a face.

"You'll make it," I tell him, hearing the hint of desperation in my voice.

"Bad news first."

"Why do you assume..."

"If it was all good, you would've led with that."

He has a point. "I can't hand over the mark. He escaped—sort of." I could still smell the ashes, sense the burst of heat, and hear the woman scream.

"You're off your game." His statement is a measure of accountability. We run a business on profit, not mistakes.

"There was a civilian in danger. I rescued her instead."

"Rescued?"

I explain the target's dance of indecision, his palpable lust when the human stumbled into his arms. I rehash my plan, the attack. "Then poof, gone. Nothing left to collect." I hold up my hands as though in proof.

Ansel's face darkens as he stares at the calendar in front of him. I picture horns sprouting from my boss's forehead. If anyone could make them look decent, it would be the son of Vikings.

"Sharon won't like this."

"She's going to rip me—you, us—a new one. I did find this, though. In the ashes." I plunk down the book.

He reaches for the leather wrapping. "Is it..."

"Don't think so. Looks like personal notes, sketches—in Latin."

"Did you try to translate?" Ansel unwraps the leather cord that holds the covers together.

"They definitely didn't teach Latin at my high school."

Ansel grunts, more caveman than anything else some days. He squints at the pages between his thumbs, stopping at the few diagrams. "I'll call Hollis. See if he can."

He extracts his phone from within a pocket and taps a few numbers. Through the tiny speaker comes a garbled voice. Ansel requests the man's presence at his earliest convenience.

If you are most people, a call from Ansel means you'd better get your ass up here before the phone disconnects. To Hollis, it could be when he damn well feels like it. Ansel knows this and lobbies for faster service. "I've got a rare single malt in from Islay, and I'm willing to share—*if* you make this a priority."

Ansel drums his fingers on the desktop, and I flop down into one of the two wingback chairs facing the desk. What does one do while waiting on a temperamental arcane shop-keeper? Attempt small talk. "Who's the greenhorn?"

He raises an eyebrow. "Downstairs? Iris. Came from Glen-dale. Some story about getting space from big city life. Why—coming out of your self-imposed cocoon?

"You first," I tease, afraid he'll sense my inner torment of the last few hours. "I'd just gotten used to Jerry. Didn't even mind when he flirted with me. Miss it now."

"He moved to Puerto Vallarta with some sugar daddy. We'll see how long this fling lasts."

Two raps at the door interrupt our banter. "Come in," Ansel says, reassembling his face into one of serious focus.

After a beat, a small man dressed like Jimmy Buffett enters. "Oof, this place is stuffy. Really, Ansel, you need some life in here. Let me bring you a few sansevierias. At least a ficus."

I push out the other chair with one foot. Ansel opens a drawer of his desk to remove a dusty bottle and two matching cut crystal glasses. He holds the bottle out to me, and I give a small shake of my head. Depending on where this conversation goes, I may need all my senses intact.

As Ansel pours, he pushes the book toward Hollis.

The spry man scoops it up and crosses an ankle over one knee. He turns the volume over in his hands, as though its wrapping could prove as important as the contents. Hollis traces the star with one finger.

Ansel hands him a glass filled with a rich, peaty liquor and leans back in his own chair to attempt the look of a man relaxed. Knowing him, he's struggling. Patience isn't a gown that ever willingly fits his frame.

Hollis takes a deep drink and closes his eyes to savor the liquid. "Burns something fierce," he says, a smile on his lips. "Absolutely stunning. How did you get it?"

"Never mind that," Ansel says, a wordless demand for information at the edge of his voice.

Hollis sips, slower this time, and again smiles in satisfaction. Reluctant, he sets the glass onto the desk and returns to the pages. After a moment, he pats at the pocket of his button up tropical shirt, then extracts a pair of reading glasses. The spectacles firmly on his nose, he again regards the text. "Hmm," he says, turning pages.

"Well—is it the book?"

Lips pursed, Hollis replies, running a finger down a page. "It appears to be something more...personal. Coordinates, some contacts, names and relationships. Associates of some kind." He flips a few more pages and frowns. He licks one finger to free a page stuck to another, then reads. "This isn't good."

Ansel leans forward in his seat, glass forgotten on the desktop. "What?"

Hollis removes his glasses to look at Ansel. "Whomever they are, they want access. *Full* access. To mine or to yours, I don't know. Maybe both."

Ansel wipes a hand down his face, then grits his teeth. "We'll be ready. I'll let Sharon know." He turns to me. "I need to catch her up to speed with the details of your evening."

I fake a dramatic sigh. Ansel's right, but I hate starting conversations with a failure—especially with my boss's boss. "Great," I say. "Can't wait."

Hollis lifts an eyebrow. "And what are those?"

I look at Ansel, who nods. We keep our cards close as a general rule, but Hollis is involved now, like it or not.

"The owner of that book didn't evaporate in a swirl of mist or dissolve into a pile of guts. He straight up burst into flames. Mean anything to you?"

Hollis blanches. "The *Fallen*."

THREE

"That's not possible. It can't be," I sputter. "Maybe vampires are real. I didn't check his teeth."

"Stuff and nonsense," Hollis counters. "Don't insult the ancients with that claptrap."

Across the desk, Ansel's face is blank, as though all the possibilities he'd considered had shattered into a million pieces at the revelation of this singular plague.

"I'm far from the oldest of my kind," Hollis begins, "but if the lore is to be believed..."

"What if he was just a fire witch?"

From his place behind the desk, Ansel shakes his head, a slow movement of denial. "Can't be."

"I know what you're thinking about what this could mean. But it doesn't. He was a loner."

"They could be like rats," Hollis says, reaching for his glass. "If there's one..."

The muscles in Ansel's jaw strain as he chews on the revelation. "If it's rats, we'll need an exterminator." He opens his desk drawer and rummages in the contents.

"I'll call Yanric," I say, crossing my arms over my chest.

"Keep this tight," Ansel says. "The barista is fine, too. But no one else."

Hollis crosses his legs in a full lotus. He rests his hands on his knees, closes his eyes, and begins to murmur words I can't decipher.

"What are you doing, old man? This isn't the time for your meditation," I say, frowning.

Hollis snaps one eye open. "If there's even the remote chance that this is true, I need to alert the coven. Now let me be." He closes the eye and returns to his incantations.

Waves of energy emit from the man. A shift from forest to sage—with a hint of scotch. I pick up the notebook and turn the pages, attempting to decipher their meaning.

"You're sure he dropped this?"

"It wasn't there before," I tell Ansel. "And it smells like him."

Hollis unfolds his legs, downs the remnants from his glass, and stands. "Your friend had plans. Big plans. And more friends. He was a scout. I'll put up new wards, and the coven will help."

"I'll call reinforcements," I say to Ansel. He stares at the red circle on the calendar, his mind far away.

∽

THE NEXT NIGHT, I'm with the others in the back room of Second Shot, a coffee shop on Montezuma. Yanric drove up from Black Canyon City, plus Grace, the owner, made three of us.

"All right boys, which weapons will I get to wield?"

I love Grace. No nonsense, funny as hell, and the best dressed barista in the southwest. Today she's paired turquoise pants with a silver mohair sweater. Her hair is a twist of a half dozen pink braids skewered with a jewel-tipped stick. There's no one like Grace.

The café in which we sit is a match for its owner. Tables and chairs built from recycled wood. Paintings from local artists cover the walls, and a rack of handmade earrings tempt customers near the register. During the daytime, the pastry case is filled with her mother's recipes for everything from mile-high slices of coffee cake to delicate eclairs. I have a personal weakness for her triple chocolate brownies.

"It's a plan, but a legitimate one. They'll arrive together. We surround them, take them out before they take one step inside."

"You're worried." Yanric's sense of smell is as tuned as my own. He runs a huge construction operation outside of Phoenix, assembling subdivisions as fast as the average kid can build a Lego tower. At night, though, he is for hire, like me. "If it's three like you say, that's one for each of us. A calm Friday night in the line of duty."

"I'm not nervous," I lie, and Yanric frowns. "All right, I'm on edge. Ansel is days away. He isn't interested in anyone—or anything—risking that."

"We'll stake out the building. Cover the square. We've got this." Grace's voice is cool, confident. With a carafe, she refills my and Yanric's mugs and joins us at the circular table.

"Hollis said he'll do some work on his end to protect the building. Straightforward job," I say, attempting to convince myself.

"We might benefit from a few...tools." Yanric downs his coffee. I swear that guy has an iron gut. "Help us control the situation."

"Keep talking."

CHAPTER
FOUR
JOAQUIN

There's something about having a motorcycle between my thighs—it disconnects my brain somehow, allowing my animal nature to take over. Instinct all but purrs within when I'm on the highway, miles disappearing beneath my wheels.

When I first bought the bike, my landlord only shook his head as he peered out his screen door at it. "You'll be smeared across the asphalt within a week. What about your future children? Heard those things are too warm for the jewels."

If only he knew children would have no part in my future, overheated balls or not.

Ahead, one of my favorite views spans the horizon. The last few miles into Sedona get me every time. Maybe it's the landscape or maybe it's that these days, I let myself get lost in beauty, soaking up a lifetime's worth.

Red rocks surround me as mountain pillars jut into bright blue skies. The desert greens of juniper, prickly pear, and agave contrast the brick, chili, and salmon-colored sandstone. Everything is gorgeous...except the tourists.

The place is crawling with them. Crammed to the hilt. People on their first horseback ride, posing for pictures like overnight rodeo stars. Others in brand new hiking boots purchased for a two-mile trail hike only to be abandoned in their apartment back home. Both types will toss plastic water bottles in the garbage like it's nothing, right before they get in their car and drive back to LA or wherever they're from. They'll post a handful of pictures that make them look like outdoorsy is their middle name and rehash their epic trip until their next fake adventure.

Yeah, I'm a little jaded.

I glide up to the stop sign, the idle rumble of my bike an eager reminder of its power. In front of me is one of those hot pink, souped-up SUVs with every window rolled down. A pair of women hang out the passenger windows and check me out like I'm part of the scenery. I won't be surprised if they ask me for a picture. Damn, this light needs to change.

One woman, her tanned cleavage an advertisement, shakes her hair and calls to me in a breathy tone. "Any advice for us on where to go tonight?" She makes no premise of trailing her gaze down me and my bike.

Giant bangle earrings dangle at her friend's ears. "Or you could just come with us. Show us around?" Caramel doe eyes watch me for interest as she gives a little wave and bites her lip.

Teresa used to bite her lip, every time I kissed a line past her belly button and down...

Honk. The car behind my bike snaps me out of my daydream and back to the land where women are too damn eager and my tolerance is too damn thin.

Without turning around, I flip the bird to the driver and shift my bike into gear. When I pass the women, I give them a two-finger wave and move my bike over the lane divider. I hear Quinn's judgement echoing in my head as I maneuver between the vehicles to take a new spot at the front. When the light turns green, I take off like a rocket.

A tidy line of buildings stretches ahead. I ease off the road and park at the back of the buildings. Along the parking lot sits a rock store, a tour guide outfit that specializes in bicycling, and a taco shop. Across the street, a small parking lot announces one of many trailheads in the area.

I take a twice-folded paper from my pocket and consult the scribbles. I navigate toward the window display of geodes, thunder eggs, and slabs of amethyst. A line of old horseshoes are nailed above the entryway, each its own ticket to good luck.

Countless tourists make the trek way out here to feel something, to see something. Read up on how to be a shaman, energize their chi, become one with the desert or some such nonsense. They want to get in touch with mythical beings, alien lifeforms, or their own future.

What they don't realize is that everything they're seeking is already here. The mail carrier, their hair stylist, that guy who always takes the good parking spot—each of them holds a secret unseen by the humans paying big money to force the issue. Sure is good for business, though.

At the door, a wave of patchouli assaults me as I step into the dim interior. The only light in the shop filters in through the large picture window.

"Welcome, my friend. Can I help you explore your ancestral plane?"

The question comes from a man dressed in a blue tracksuit. He wears sunglasses indoors and a dozen silver bangles along one arm. Incense does little to mask the stench of unwashed pits and fried food. He regards me a moment, eyebrows drawing together. "Get in touch with your ancestors, perhaps?"

"Nope," I say, peering into boxes, fingering the stones in a basket of jasper.

The man crosses his arms, holding one elbow in the opposite hand. "You have an incredible aura," he says, flapping his hand around in front of me. "Lavender with a golden sparkle."

"I assure you, I'm anti-glitter."

"Pity," he says, pressing his lips together. "Let me know if you have any questions."

"Yanric said you could help me get a few things I need."

The name drop catches his attention. He scans the shop for other customers before closing the shop door and flipping the sign to closed. With a jerk of his chin, he indicates a doorway over which dangles a beaded curtain. "So you can...make your selection in private." I nod and follow him to the back storage area, a maze of shelving and precarious stacks. "What are we after? We're decently stocked at the moment. Just got a shipment in from the DR."

I snag a box from the nearest shelf and peer inside. A dozen fossilized trilobites jostle in the cardboard confines. "I need the...celestial variety."

He reaches for some boxes, stacks them in his arms. The man turns to meet my eyes. His glow, a faint indigo. Gentry. "Really? What level are we talking?"

"Top. Pretty close to the tippy top—we think. Just want to be prepared. You know, in case."

"I see." He checks a filing cabinet's drawers and extracts a necklace with a modest pendant.

"It's ugly." I dangle the thing, frowning. "And there's a hole in it."

"Adderstone. Helps you discern tricks or disguises. Might buy you time if nothing else."

"Neat. But say we want to...kill."

The man purses his lips and regards me. "Haven't seen that kind of action here in centuries. Millenia. Everything is a guess, you see."

"We want to be ready for any threat."

"Of course." He reaches for a wooden box over my shoulder. He lifts a sheath from within, the hilt of a dagger protruding from its top, and hands it to me. "Won't kill, but will wound, distract. Help you sort out who is friend and who is...foe. Come back next week, and I'll see what else I can dig up."

The hilt is a whorl of silver and black. "I'll take what I can get," I say. I slide the blade from the sheath. "It's broken!"

He shrugs. "Fix it. Or stab with the jagged end."

I frown and tuck the piece of junk in my pocket. "How much?"

"On the house," he says, "for a trade."

The hair on the back of my neck stands. Abuela warned me never to make deals with *las hadas*. I give him a wary look, reaching again for the damaged weapon.

"ETA?"

"Excuse me?"

"When will they get here?"

I debate a lie, then dismiss the urge. Mama didn't raise a fool. "Not sure. Friday, maybe."

"Friday is now," he says, his eyes on the window.

FIVE

LOTTE

T he cliffside stretches out ahead of me as I sit on the edge. I make slow circles with my ankles, stiff in my hiking boots. Leaning back, hands behind to prop me up, I tip my chin to the sky, bright blue and cloudless. Two buzzards circle its depths. I inhale the fresh air and fill my lungs before exhaling a controlled breath. I push myself up and rummage in my daypack for lunch.

I withdraw a short stack of pita bread, avocado, and a tub of cashew spread a customer brought me. I scoop a blob of the dip with a pita triangle. *Not bad.* The red pepper blend would go well with a Malbec. Maybe I'll take the long way home, stop by that winery in Jerome.

Sunbeams warm my scalp as I fish for the small pocket knife I keep in my pocket. A Christmas gift from one of my sisters, an insult I'd shrugged off and added to my hiking gear. The blade makes quick work of the avocado, slicing the smooth green fruit. I arrange snacks on top of a rock before extracting a paperback. I flip open to my bookmark. A friendship bracelet, half knotted, slips into my lap, and I dive back into the story in which a pioneer girl lives in a home dug from the side of a hill. I was at the part where one of the family's oxen punctured the ceiling with a wayward hoof.

There were so many childhood books I'd missed out on. I

loved little more than indulging myself in catching up. The heroine of these books is spirited, independent. She uses her moral compass as her guide. These things, I wanted for myself, had always wanted.

Light shifts on the massive rock faces on the horizon. Their colors darken to something imminent, promising. While I'd been lost on the banks of Plum Creek, the day had pressed on with its agenda.

As the pre-twilight chill tickles my neck, I retrieve the friendship bracelet from my lap. I anchor it between the pages and tuck the novel back inside my bright orange pack. The buzzards settle on a telephone wire in the distance. I take a deep swig from my water bottle and pack it, too. After a tug on the drawstring, I shoulder my pack and head out.

I take in the sight ahead of me, a rainbow of rocks, spectacular in their magnitude. With an inhale, I take it in, close my eyes, and ask for guidance. Forgiveness.

But no answer comes. How can one redeem themselves, atone for sins, with little understanding of the pathway to light? Guess prayer won't work today.

In front of me, a small canyon heads west, beckoning my return through the quiet landscape. Birds and rabbits flit and hop about, seeking cover and warmth. In the distance, a shape slips between the scrub bushes. Coyote, maybe. Or puma.

I stamp my feet to bring sensation back to my toes and blow on my fingertips. With no blanket of clouds, cold rushes in as the sun sets, a bitter runner up.

Voices rise and fall as the parking lot comes into view. I pause at the picnic table. A bunch of guys laugh and joke, tossing insults like confetti at a parade. I know the type.

When you run a small business in a tourist town, you get used to dealing with the public. Add because I'm a woman and some treat me like an incompetent flower, I condition myself to ignore the worst.

Still, godsdamnit, a girl should get a break on her day off.

The trio crowds around a dark silver sedan, a case of cheap beer on the hood. They face west, here for the show of oranges and purples set to streak the sky. The edge of their conversation reaches me as one of them recounts his conquest the night before.

"An ass like a ripe peach. It was spectacular. She bounced on my lap until I couldn't see straight."

"I met a guy whose mouth was silk." The second one sighs and rests his chin in one hand. "Pretty sure I passed out a time or two."

The third listens, straight-faced, and shakes his head. "Someone else is sitting watch tonight. I'll find the hottest piece in town."

"Not it," says the first guy. "I promised her I'd be back for round two."

The second guy groans and reaches for another can. "Bagging the same human doesn't count. It's quantity, not quality."

From behind the boulder, I roll my eyes. *Gross.*

First Guy raises an eyebrow. "Fine. Let's make a bet."

Second and Third high-five each other. "You're on."

I shift positions, seeking an escape. A group of assholes will never come between me and inner peace—or whatever it is the guidebooks say I'm trying to achieve out here.

Crouched low, I sneak around the boulders, edging the lot to avoid their attention. I fumble for the key to my bike lock with one hand while I zip up my jacket with the other and make a beeline for my bike chained near the shops.

A latent cottontail zigzags across my path. I trip trying to avoid the panicked beast. My knee bashes into a rock and I swear. At the sound, three heads turn my way.

"Who have we here?" The first of the group scrutinizes me and his eyes narrow. He wears a flannel over a waffle-weave shirt, a trucker's hat perched over his thinning hair.

The second one, in a green, puffy coat, removes his sunglasses to appraise me. A slow smile spreads across his face. "Hel-lo."

The third watches, his hands tight around a beer can. He finishes the contents, watching me, then crushes the can underneath a foot. Heavy logging boots collapse the aluminum like an insect. "You here alone?"

"First one back," I say. "Going to make dinner for the gang."

The first guy makes a show of looking around the empty parking lot. "Are you sure they are still here?"

He had me there.

The third slips behind me. He stands too close. Heat flushes against the back of my thighs and along my neckline. He leans over my shoulder to whisper in my ear. "I don't think you have anyone with you," he says. "I think you were all alone."

I take a few steps away and ease my hand into my pocket. My fingers close around the handle of the knife. I clench my other fist. Pinpricks shoot against the inside of my palm as my fingertips spark, muted for the moment.

"We were hoping to make some friends," the first guy says. He jumps down from the tabletop. "We're new in town and looking for a place to stay. Know anyone renting out their place?"

I glance over his shoulder at the small stretch of shops across the street. This late in the day, most windows are shuttered, the employees long gone.

I calculate the time it would take to run to my bike, unlock the chain, and—ride off? With three of them and one of me, the odds aren't in my favor.

The first of them turns his head to follow my gaze, then addresses me again. "Boys, I don't think our new friend trusts us."

"But we've been nothing but charming," says the second.

"Why don't you take us to your place?" The third strolls toward me, hands in pockets. "Perhaps we could get to know each other, become friends. You could invite your hiking buddies, too, you know."

I back away, only to find the second behind me again. They back me up against their car and time slows. I rub my fingertips together, readying my response. With a shake of my hair, I summon the goddess as energy pulses deep within my core.

A rumble breaks the silence as a motorcycle emerges from behind the buildings. Dust coats the air as the driver spins the bike in a quarter circle in the dirt.

The rider removes his helmet, and for a moment, I forget to breathe. *Fates preserve us.* Dark, satin hair shakes out, framing his face in long layers. Coal black eyes focus first on me, as though checking for injury, then assesses each of my obnoxious and volatile groupies before returning to me. "Ma'am, your party sent me to find you. I'm supposed to tell you they are waiting—and hungry."

"Thank you," I say, blood rushing back to my hands.

"How about I give you a ride?"

I nod, grateful. My bike can wait. I turn to the creeps. "Good luck finding a room," I say, approaching the motorcycle.

Creep Number Two grumbles. The third turns his back to me and reaches for another beer. The first, however, watches me like a hawk tracking a mouse.

The second I'm behind the stranger on the bike, I realize a moment too late that he could be as dangerous, if not more so, than the group I'll be leaving behind. He starts the engine and we're off.

A mile down the road, he slows the bike and pulls over to the side. Both hands on the handlebars, he twists around on the seat.

"If you hop off and dig in the cargo box, there's a second helmet," he says. "Didn't have the time back there."

I slide off the bike, my tush warm from the ride. In the cargo box is a black helmet, an ancient knife tucked underneath. *Looks like the...but it can't be.* I say nothing as I mount the bike and place the helmet on my head. My fingers fumble at the clips.

He turns to adjust my straps and I stare unabashed in my excuse of proximity. A 5 o'clock shadow crosses his jawline. I drink in my closeness to a man under the guise of safety adjustments.

Practiced, he fits the helmet below my chin, then gives a nod of satisfaction. "Not any good if it slips off and you crack your head open."

"Again, thanks for this."

"Of course." He looks at me, deciding. "It isn't safe to be out here by yourself. At least not without...protection. Those guys weren't typical jerks."

An unspoken explanation sits in the air between us. I wait for more.

"Maybe stay away from guys like that." He raises an eyebrow as though seeking confirmation.

"Guess I'll have to take your word that I didn't trade one danger for another," I say.

He breaks out in a toothy grin. "That was your second mistake."

CHAPTER

SIX

JOAQUIN

"Who was she?"

"She?"

"The woman who made you late," Ansel says. He taps on a tablet, entering an order. "Two pints of the amber and a set of darts. Couple in the hats," he calls to the bartender, who busies herself with the glasses.

Morgan's was slammed for a weekday. While the tourist season ebbs after the holidays, a good pub remains a central gathering place.

Customers out of earshot, Ansel slides a glass my way. "Since a romp in the sheets isn't part of the report, what's the bad news?"

"They're here."

Recognition flashes behind his eyes and he blinks. "Already? Godsdamnit!" He pounds his fist onto the bar. Two patrons jump in their seats, startled.

I tell him about the beer cans, the sedan. The girl—no, woman—and their interest in her. "Like cats playing with a cornered mouse."

"She's lucky you were there," Ansel says. "Both of you could've been killed."

"Harder to do than one may think." I lift my glass and sprinkle salt from the shaker on my napkin.

Ansel watches me. "For a man who lives outdoors ninety-eight percent of the time, you sure get fancy."

"I don't like it when glasses stick," I say, shrugging. "Did Sharon send over any details?"

Ansel sighs. He places both hands on the bar and hangs his head. "Confirmation. Or at least a solid likelihood based on those she knew before. She wants an ID."

"It's not like they wear nametags."

"Then we'll have to get it out of them another way. What do we know so far?" Ansel makes a formidable enemy. He analyzes like a man with nothing else to do and nowhere else to be. Technically, both are true, but still.

"They get their kicks off intimidation," I say as I remember the hiker. From afar, I'd seen short, dark hair, hiking boots, and those impractical leggings women wear like pants.

Not that I'm complaining about her legs alongside mine. On the bike, she'd maintained a loose hold around my waist. At abrupt stops, inertia pressed her breasts against my back. That brief contact was enough to create an ache, a need for an ice cold shower.

I'd recognized the woman the moment I saw her, though I doubt she knows me. I'd watched her lock up the candle shop countless times. Funny how you can lead parallel lives with someone for so long, then one day—bam!—you see them everywhere.

But it wasn't until I was next to her on the bike, adjusting that strap with her violet eyes inches from mine, that I had the urge to reach out and brush a finger along her cheek. Twirl a lock of hair. The gut-wrenching impulse to kiss a woman, melt into the slight pressure of her mouth, hot against my own. This woman emitted a wild energy, something feral and ancient. I'd wanted to taste it. Curl up inside, revel in the heat.

I'd dropped her off by the square. I hadn't wanted to be the guy who watched her walk away, but I did. Every second I could. She was smoking hot, with an animal stride that caught the attention of more than me.

I reached for the little toothpick holder on the bar to

address my canines, thinking. She hadn't seemed scared, not of those jerks or of me. Not really. She was capable, held the stance of a wildcat, ready to pounce, yet somehow...reluctant.

Maybe it's my line of work but I seek motives. A thought process can run through your brain, causing hormones to light up every cell in your body, and yet no one around you seems to notice. But I will.

A hint of curiosity. I wanted to know her. Find out what made her tick. What made her purr.

"A disaster waiting to happen. We should have anticipated this." Ansel had continued to talk while I'd been miles away, lost in that lavender gaze. "Sharon chewed my ass—" I raised an eyebrow, and he shot me a look. "Not in that way."

"We should draw them out. Make them come to us. They have an affinity for competition. Oh, and things that are sharp." I spot the couple from earlier across the room, deep into their second beers and a round of Cricket. "How about darts?"

He glares at me. "This isn't a game."

"Think about it. We hold a contest. Make it big. They'll come."

"Just because they show up doesn't mean we'll be able to do anything about them."

"We can gather intel if nothing else."

"I don't have a better plan," he admits, then works his jaw, considering. "Might be good for business. I'll think about it."

"Saturday night?"

He nods. "Hollis called. He translated more of the book."

"And?" I finish the dregs of my beer and reach for a menu I have memorized.

"He said there are plans for an organization. Structures. Something about a reorientation of the stars."

"Probably code," I say, rubbing at my chin.

"Could be. I told him you'd pick it up, get the details."

"I'll go see what he found." I can never eat with questions hanging in the air. "But there better be a burger waiting when I get back."

~

I CLATTER down the stairs from Ansel's office, push out the back door of Morgan's, and head out into the atrium. Constructed as an accidental gap as the buildings around the block filled in, this space at their center serves as a refuge for the shop owners, a pit stop for hummingbirds, and a little piece of calm in the center of a growing city. Benches wrap around a tree planted long before any of our lifetimes. Gnarled trunk and gangly branches, its tips stretch toward the slice of sky above.

Most residents do not know this pocket of peace exists. The few who do guard the knowledge like a secret.

Someone has run an extension cord from their building to a small fountain placed near the benches. Party lights hang across the atrium. My pigeon buddies peck at a scattering of seed. I need to spend more time out here.

At the back door to Hollis's shop, a bell jingles as I enter. Oxygen and moist air fill my lungs. As my eyes adjust to the lush, overgrown inside of the shop, I search for the owner within the urban jungle.

My knee catches the leg of a table covered in tiny succulents, and I wince. The rainbow of offerings sit in rows of matching pots. Interspersed among them, tiny cacti offer their prickly, rounded selves to a grow light angled over the collection like a private sun.

A small shelf divides one wall near the cash register. On the shelf sits a trio of photographs. One is of Hollis on a windswept moor. He wears a bright tangerine raincoat and green galoshes, a lopsided grin on his face. In one hand, he holds a goblet up to the rainy sky. In the other, a walking stick keeps him upright on the boggy ground. The second photograph features a tiny farmhouse with navy shutters, a cow out front. A long, low rock wall lines the foreground, and a bouquet of wildflowers lies abandoned in the driveway. The third frame features a little girl in a swing, eyes squeezed shut against the sunlight on her face, mid-laugh, feet kicking up toward the clouds.

"Welcome," comes a voice at my side. "Interested in sprucing up that lair of yours?"

"The day I give a damn about plants, you'll be the first to know."

"Then you must be here for the book."

I nod. In the last two minutes, I've said more to Hollis than I have in the last two years. While there isn't specific animosity between him and my boss, there's some history, and my loyalty has a simple line. Still, he's helping us. "Thanks for translating. What did you find?"

"I'll show you," he says, and turns to address his shop. "Now, where did I leave that thing?"

I shuffle a few steps to make room for the man as he hunts through the shop. He lifts stacks of invoices, peeks behind pots. I bite back a retort about not letting precious evidence out of one's sight and occupy my thoughts instead.

For a guy short on time, I can wait like the best of them. Near the front window, my eyes search the square from habit, lingering over each passerby. A rainbow of sweaters and hats shuffle by. Shopping bags in some hands, dog leashes in others. Across the square, I note that the lights in the candle shop are on.

"Aha!" Hollis exclaims, holding the book aloft. He presses it to my chest and lowers his voice. "I put it under the jade. Dry and lucky. Tell that boss of yours not to let this out of his sight. It's full of old magic and dark plans."

I grimace at the book, holding it out with two fingers. "What does it say?"

"What do you know of the White Amulet?"

I shake my head. "Nothing."

"Better that way." Hollis rips several sheets from a yellow legal pad near the register. He folds them in half and hands them to me. "My notes, the translations. They're coming, that's for certain. What our world will look like when they do? Now that's the question."

CHAPTER
SEVEN
LOTTE

When you live alone for too long, you pick up awkward habits. My own never bother me until someone else points them out.

This afternoon I plaited my hair into dozens of tiny braids, bit off every nail I could chew, and left my used tea bags on the counter. Even I didn't want to be my roommate. Today I'd be extra annoying since I'd spent the evening trying to forget the heat of his body against mine. The smell of his cologne—cedar and vetiver—and the way he ran a finger across his lower lip when thinking.

These thoughts lingered long after he'd dropped me off. They stoked a fire in my belly, made me wonder what he would have done if I'd run my hands along his biceps, across his abs, lower...

Two old ladies mutter about the chill in the shop on their way out, snapping me back to the present. I didn't bother to tell them I'd cranked up the AC so I wouldn't sweat through my silky blouse, a stupid wardrobe choice when my inner fires raged.

"You'll never make friends this way," I say aloud to the empty store and sigh. "Let alone..." I put on a mock, posh accent. "Excuse me, sir. Could you possibly pull over this motorcycle? The engine's running warm and I'm a bit distracted by my desire to rip your clothes off."

He'd been so...nice. He'd looked out for me, a stranger. Talked to me. It had been too long since I'd held a conversation longer than the need to complete a transaction. He'd *seen* me, even if it had taken a run-in with rejects to make it happen.

Loneliness isn't good for anyone. You collect those tiny spoons, restaurant matchbooks, or cats. Talk to yourself in ridiculous accents. Freeze the other half of every meal you make.

I can see my future now. The shop will get dusty from the lack of customers willing to placate an old crone. I'll wither away until one day when they want to tear down this building and make way for a skyscraper, here I'll be sitting, friendless and forgotten.

Customers breeze through the door, disrupting my pity party. I wrap my newest braid behind one ear and will a smile across my face. No time like the present to fake it until I make it.

The women hustle over to the tables. Their mass market, puffy coats are bright gems in my shop of neutrals. Red, cobalt, hunter, and silver. Knitted hats over salon-streaked hair. They shoulder matching tote bags, and their pores reek of Pinot Noir.

A wine weekend with the girls. *Great.* Cue return of pity party.

I watch the women weave through the shop. A petite woman with a gold pendant spelling *Roseanne* in cursive, passes over the table of vanilla and pine scented jars to aim for the tropical section. Two others follow her while one lingers at the table dotted with pinecones among my forest collection.

With a flash of a smile none of them notice, I retreat to my stool behind the counter. The coward's way.

The three in the corner busy themselves with tequila sunrise and mango paradise. They hold candles under their noses and sniff in comparison. In a different circumstance, I would suggest they smell the lids for the best scent.

Now, I am all observation, sales be damned. I'll watch like a proper voyeur.

The women move on to a table crowded with seashells and stones I collected in Greece. Roseanne hoists a candle from the table. It's blue, with a scent I named Ocean Shores. "Smells like my honeymoon. Maybe we need a return for our anniversary. Twenty years come August."

Her friend makes a show of putting a fingertip to each temple and closing her eyes. "I see long walks on the beach, a bottle of ouzo, and lots of sex."

The third woman's eyes widen, and she exchanges her matching candle with a different one. Sunny Sands—safe.

Roseanne notices. "Aw, come on Jess. Wouldn't you like to spice things up a bit at home? Reconnect with your younger years and all. Where did you and Amahl honeymoon?"

"P-P-Palm Springs. His aunt has a house there."

"Was she home?" Roseanne winks, and Jess's cheeks pink from the attention. "What I wouldn't give for a week at the beach with no kids. We take what we can get, though, right? Happy weekend, girls. Candles and daydreams are on me."

"Are you all celebrating?" Sometimes I can't help myself from asking the obvious. Drawing out the conversation is the quiet desperation of a lonely shopkeeper.

"Girls' weekend," says the woman cradling a Tea & Roses candle in her hands.

"Sounds like fun," I say, willing my envy to abate.

One woman accepts her bagged candle from me and addresses the group. "What are we doing tonight?"

Roseanne pulls out her phone while I finish scanning her candles. "We have dinner at that adorable Mexican restaurant down the block at six. Then...drinks? Dancing?"

"Karaoke?"

"I can't sing," Jess says.

"No one at those places can sing, that's the point."

"It's our last night. I say we cruise Whiskey Row. When in

Prescott and all. Besides, we've got a long plane ride tomorrow during which to regret our decisions. Might as well make it a good night."

Roseanne is flicking her finger along her phone screen, consulting the contents. "There's a dart competition at the bar."

My ears perk up.

Jess asks, "Which bar?"

"The one with that hot bartender. The one who looks like he could throw you over his shoulder and spank the Sunday out of you."

Jess puts a hand to her mouth. "Roseanne!"

I know the very one. His friend isn't half bad, either. And he has a bike.

"Oh yeah," says their other friend, a brunette with a silver streak in her curls. "I liked him."

"Thank you," Roseanne says as she accepts the bag from me, my logo stamped on the front. "Let's drop these off at the rental. What does one wear to a dart contest?"

"As little as possible?"

The women burst into laughter as they exit the shop. As they step out the door, I know two things to be true.

One, I want that. The friendship, the camaraderie, the trust, and the teasing.

Two, I have plans for tonight.

When I duck in through the front door, I make my way to the back of the pub and brace myself against the wall.

I don't love crowds. Someone like me avoids places in which they can be cornered. But tonight, I need people. I need a reminder of my choices and their consequences. I need humanity.

After I closed the shop, I'd nipped up to my apartment and assessed my outfit. My closet fits the needs of two women: upscale shop owner with neutrals in muted, dusty colors, and the black of a nocturnal animal. Somehow, neither seemed the right fit for a night of sports, so I settled for a combination. Black leather pants and a faded lavender T-shirt tucked in at my waist. Subtle black flats stand in for my favorite black boots. I'd unbraided my earlier creations, freeing my tresses, and added a black scarf around my neck. I give off edgy balle-rina vibes, which is all I'm willing to risk tonight.

I refuse to lie to myself, to pretend this isn't an opportunity to be close to him. In the hours before the women walked into my shop, I'd watched him enter and exit the bar a half dozen times. There is no guarantee he'll still be here, but I'm here on hope. Riding behind him on his motorcycle did something to my insides. Sent a thrill to my core. I want that feeling again, if only for a moment.

Spend too much time alone, and you forget to feel. Forget the power someone—like a stranger with impossibly dark eyes and sexy lips—can have on you. It's intoxicating, and I've been sober far too long.

The contest is in full swing when I enter. I spot the afore-mentioned bartender behind the bar. He watches the crowd, assessing everyone. Employees I don't know run circles around him, handing out drinks, making change, yelling and joking with the patrons. Ansel remains still, brow furrowed as hopeful contestants vie for top scores.

In the corner booth sits my candle crew. Several empty pint glasses and a plate of fries lay abandoned on the table. Roseanne looks over to the bar at Ansel then back at her friends. She whispers and waggles her eyebrows, and they break out into laughter. I swallow, wishing I knew the secret.

I shouldn't have come. Foolish in my suburban outfits and reclusive ways, I knew that, in getting closer to people who live a typical life, I'd feel further away. Hanging my head, I push past a few bodies on my way to the exit, more laughing and jostling with buddies I'll never have, when I hear a voice at the microphone.

"For our last qualifying round, we have Wesley, the butcher..."

I recognize his voice as the crowd cheers. The rich tenor of sound reminds me of my rescue, his concern.

I reverse course and shoulder my way closer to the front. Being smaller can be convenient as you fit in tinier places.

When I duck around a flannel-clad elbow, I'm in front of a makeshift stage. My rescuer stands before the duct tape-outlined firing lanes. Wesley, or the man I assume to be the butcher, holds three darts aloft. The tips glint in the overhead lights, his flights striped with blue and green.

The announcer on whom I turn all my attention turns to a man at his left. "We have Ronnie, your favorite baker and mine, in spot two. Came to Morgan's straight from work, I see."

The crowd claps for Ronnie, who puts his hand over his heart and takes a bow. He pulls darts from the front pocket of an apron emblazoned with *Honey Cakes.*

"There's room for one more contestant in our last heat. I'll even let you use my lucky Arachnids." The announcer scans the crowd, waiting for a volunteer. "Speak now or forever hold your peace."

There are moments when you do something with half your brain before the other half, the more reasonable half, catches up and kicks you in the butt. This is one of them.

My hand shoots up and my mouth says, "I'm in," before my rational self can stop that train from leaving the station.

The announcer's eyes seek my voice out in the crowd, then rest on me, stunned, as he registers my claim.

"Go on up there," a kind voice says at my side. An older man in a newsboy cap nudges me. "If you win," he says, "the next beer is on me."

"Let's welcome our final contestant." The announcer holds out a small case and leans toward me as I make my way to the last lane. His lips all but brush my cheek as he whispers away from the microphone. "What was your name, miss...?"

I look into his eyes, and for a moment, the room is still. The pull between us is electric, pulsing. My fingers itch, shooting a purple spark at his feet.

I blink and time restarts, the crowd shuffling and murmuring with impatience. "Lotte," I say into the microphone, startling at the sound of my voice. "And I brought my own darts." I extract a case from my jacket.

"Joaquin," he says, away from the microphone. He smiles a moment longer before turning back to the crowd.

I melt into a puddle of need then and there. Holding a dart might be beyond my capabilities.

"Your turn—Lotte."

∼

AFTER A HANDFUL OF ROUNDS, it was obvious Ronnie should stick to his day job. He was cheery, though, and got plenty of free advertising for the bakery. When his score lagged over triple digits, he bowed to me and the butcher before withdrawing from the contest.

The butcher was a tougher opponent, but when a tip hit the metal of the outer ring and the dart rebounded, I solidified my win with a treble shot. When he shook my hand, he added in a hushed tone, "Don't let those assholes win. It's all on you," and headed for the barstool next to the baker.

"We'll take a ten-minute break to allow our finalists to make their way up here and for everyone to get another round." He turns to me and adds, "Nice shots...Lotte." He winks and my stomach somersaults.

Anxious at his and the crowd's sudden attention, I wave off the offers of a drink. I lean back against the wall and spend copious energy attempting to look relaxed. The bartender remains in statue form. In fairness, he makes a good one: classic jawline, perfect nose, broad shoulders of a demigod. He is a rock in the sea of humanity flowing around him.

"Hello again. Almost didn't recognize you without hiking boots."

I whirl to find a face I'd never wanted to see again. He takes his time, sliding his gaze up my body.

Gross. I wish I could attribute disgusting behavior to one species or another, but I can't.

Assholes are universal.

I clench my hands into fists, squeezing the dart shafts in an attempt to remain calm. "Awfully brazen of you to be here. What happened—didn't get enough rejection back home?" In the interim from that day on the trail, I'd figured out exactly who I'd been dealing with. Why here, and why now, was still a mystery I couldn't toy with in front of this crowd.

"That's the pot calling the kettle black," he tells me as a Cheshire grin spreads across his face. "Might be fun to have you as a competitor." He spreads an array of neon tipped darts in front of me, empty eyes of the heartless behind. In a sweater so new there was still a crease down its center, he plays the part of tourist well. Cologne sweetens the air, and my fingertips itch to touch the throat it graces. Will he be cold to the touch or are the rumors true? All necks are vulnerable.

A speaker on the wall crackles to life. "Two minutes! If I can have Rowan, Thad, and Lotte to the front."

I stare hard into my opponent's eyes, seeking reason, motive, or rationale. There I see darkness but little form. I drop my gaze. Not here, not now. "I'm here to have fun," I say, slowing the blood in my veins, willing my pulse to calm.

Long ago, on a lost summer afternoon, one of my sisters found a snake among the tall grasses. The animal curled around her arm and across her shoulders before returning to its business, leaving streaks of shimmering gold on her bare forearms.

"Why do you let it crawl on you?" I'd asked. "Aren't you afraid?"

"The thing about serpents," she'd said, "is that you're far safer when you watch them, keep them close by. Ignore them and they'll watch you, waiting to strike."

Now, in the crowded bar smelling of stale fried foods, pheromones, and now something ancient and elemental, I grit my teeth, determined to keep my eyes on the snake. "Good luck," I say, and hold out my hand to my opponent.

"Not falling for that one."

Beyond our awareness, the crowd has resumed its watch of the stage and our exchange becomes front and center. The masses boo his rejection, unable to hear him but in full view of the refusal to take my proffered hand.

"Sportsmanship is paramount in this establishment," Joaquin says into the microphone, the edge of his voice a veiled threat.

A muscle below my opponent's eye twitches and he clasps my hand. I see a flash of imagery, white on gray on black. I inhale, and he drops my hand, shaking out his own.

The third finalist, a frat-boy type, lumbers over, hand held high. "May the best man...er woman...win."

Seemingly harmless. He winks as I high-five him. Cue eye roll.

"Same rules," my dark-haired comrade tells us. "Coin toss put Thad up first."

I parcel out names when the younger man steps forward.

So, my antagonist is Rowan.

We play, each of us scoring with regularity. Thad is decent but inconsistent. When Rowan and I dip below 171, Thad is sunk.

"Three darts stand between these two and a possible win." Joaquin points to the scoreboard. "Lotte is sitting pretty at 167, but Rowan has more options at 147." He meets my eyes and continues, "But the thing about darts is it's still anyone's game."

"You're not bad," Rowan says. He walks behind, considering his target. "But I'm better. You may have the sight, but I've had longer to practice." His words were a hiss in my ear. He steps to the line and takes a deep breath, exhaling through his nostrils. He tosses. Triple twenty. The crowd roars, and he lifts both his hands in the air to encourage their fever. "Suck it!"

Rowan's friend from the trailhead has pushed his way to the front. He high fives those around him and cheers. I spot his other friend making his way through the crowd, using both hands to hold three pint glasses between his fingers. I see the bartender lift an eyebrow at Joaquin.

The friend with the beers passes one to Rowan who downs it. He wipes his mouth with the back of his hand, then shakes himself from shoulders to toes. "Let's do this!"

Triple seventeen.

Again, the volume rises and Rowan bows for the crowd. Across the room, the bartender glowers and tells a server something no one else can hear. She blanches and runs off.

Rowan throws again. Eighteen. Single.

The crowd makes an audible wince, then I sense the sudden weight of all eyes on me.

"Go ahead," Rowan says, sweeping his hand toward the dartboard. "You could get lucky. Then again, you could bow out now, save face."

"I could," I say. I allow myself a moment of pity. Give myself permission to wallow in the idea that luck has never been, nor will it ever be, my life. Luck didn't land me in this town, pandering to visitors, envious of book clubs and baby showers while pining after a man who sees me as a damsel in distress. There is no game of chance in my reality, no intangible entity on which to blame this life, this moment.

But I am playing a part, escaping my reality for the briefest of evenings. No one knows me, and I can choose my pathway, if just for the next few minutes. Later, I will withdraw to my self-made cloister and atone for ever daydreaming to begin with.

For now, I am frustrated and lonely. Ticked off that this celestial creep can live his best life while I am afforded crumbs. Here and now, I don't give a damn who sees the fire in my blood.

"Rowan," I say, and mutter, "if that's your real name," under my breath. He flares his nostrils and glares at me. I ignore him. "You're fairly decent yourself." I make a show of checking that the shafts and barrels are tight, my hot pink flights intact.

I ordered the darts on a whim when I uncovered an old

cork board left by my shop's former occupant. The repetitive *thwack* of metal to cork has been my nightly practice for more evenings than I care to count.

I step to the line, careful of my foot placement. "I appreciate your chivalrous offer to claim the title so I needn't look bad in front of all these fine people." Whistles call to me from the back. I continue, "Thing is, you wear overconfidence like a second skin."

Rowan glowers as the faces of his friends freeze, their mouths open. I turn and appraise the scoreboard. "Your fatal flaw is a failure to assess the competition. You never asked if this was my first tourney. Or how long I've been playing."

I see the bartender uncross his arms and place his hands on the bar top. He leans forward as though waiting for the moment the contest ends.

Joaquin's eyes haven't left me. He, too, draws closer, as though ready to spring into action. The surrounding crowd goes quiet.

"Had you bothered to get to know me, to know your—*competition*," I say, enunciating the word, "you would know I grew up with sisters who just so happen to love a competition. Any competition. You name it, we bet on it, whether to assign chores or choose lovers." I wink at the crowd and many laugh. Others push at the bodies to get closer to the drama.

Rowan's eyes narrow and he crosses his arms.

"You would have learned that we came up with all manner of ways to one-up each other, each fighting to be on top. Darts, races, hand-to-hand combat. Makes for a scrappy upbringing."

The audience chuckles, and I smirk, then reach to untie the scarf from around my neck. I hand it to Joaquin who stares at me, incredulous. I nod, and he blinks twice before stepping behind me with the scarf.

As people in the crowd translate his next movements, they gasp.

Blindfold in place, I smile at the crowd. "You see, it's never about luck, Rowan. It's about the fate you deserve." I pause for a deep breath and turn toward the board. I picture it like a wheel of fortune, with choices and intersecting destinies in front of me. I think of its center, of where I want to be, and steel my heart.

"If you knew me," I say to Rowan and anyone else who is listening, judging, and doubting, "you would know I believe in reaping what we sow. That we earn our lot in life, wielding weapons we fashion with our words and deeds."

With a final exhale, I release one dart after the other. Each flies fast, silent, and true.

Shouts and cheers erupt in the bar as I push the fabric off my eyes.

Triple twenty, triple twenty, bullseye.

The microphone is limp in Joaquin's hand, his eyes wide.

"She cheated! I saw her." Rowan's words are a furious challenge.

Not waiting to learn of my prize, I press into the crowd.

The older gentleman from earlier tugs at my sleeve as I brush past. "That was amazing! Hey, wait, I promised you a beer."

"Another time," I say, and beeline for the door. A rush of cold air meets my cheeks, and my breath is visible in big puffs. Adrenaline from the win courses through my veins. I step onto the pavement when I hear shouts behind. I quickstep across the asphalt. Should have gone with the boots.

"Stop," Rowan yells from behind me. "Or are you admitting your guilt?"

On the grass of the square, I study my surroundings. I could hide, but where? And for how long?

"Are you threatening one of my patrons?"

I whip around and see the bartender on the sidewalk, Joaquin next to him.

"So what if I am? What is a halfborn like you going to do about it?"

"Not a damn thing. You're the one who's going to back his ass out of here if you have any sense," Joaquin counters.

"When we find out what you're doing here," the bartender

says, his voice a measured calm, "in my town without my permission, you will have earned what's coming for you."

"Here's news for you," Rowan says, as his friends exit the bar to flank him on the sidewalk. "You don't own this place. You don't get to decide who is and isn't allowed to be here."

"You'll have your date with destiny, and I intend to be around to witness." The bartender crosses his arms and dares their response. "Or you could just leave. See how that works out for you. Either way, consider this my polite warning to pack your shit and hit the road."

Rowan shakes his head and laughs. "You know, for a second there, I thought you might bring some actual heat. Guess I was wrong. You're just some juiced-up halfborn with an overpaid bouncer."

Joaquin and his boss bristle, but the latter gives a short shake of his head. A warning to ignore the taunts.

"Come on, boys, we've got the whole night ahead of us." They move down the sidewalk, laughing and pushing each other, before Rowan calls to me. "Be seeing you, princess," he adds, and blows me a kiss. "Count on it."

"Joaquin?" The bartender's voice is icy, a warning.

"Yeah?"

"Let them go. Instead, escort our winner home." He presses an envelope into Joaquin's hand.

Joaquin nods at his boss, then jogs to catch up with me. "May I walk you home?"

"I suppose," I say. "But we're halfway there, already." In my haste to escape, I'd drawn into the trees, their massive trunks looming above. "We won't even have time for a proper introduction."

The corner of his mouth turns up. "Then I'll make it fast."

EIGHT

JOAQUIN

For the record, never tell a woman you'll make anything fast. Unless she asks for it that way. Then make it quick, and make it rough. Up against the wall, on the desk, or on a bearskin rug.

Any other time? Draw. It. Out.

But I digress.

Lotte didn't want, and somewhat resented, my forced chivalry. I could see it in the way her lips pressed together at Ansel's insistence she be escorted. She attempted to breeze past her bitterness with lighthearted banter, but I can tell when a woman wants to be alone.

It's not personal, and it's not like I'm attracted to weak-willed women.

She tolerates my company the length of the square. When we draw near her shop, she stops. "There's my door. I've got this."

I pause on the sidewalk. What did I hope would happen? That she'd invite me up to her place. Put on some coffee. We'd stay up all night, talking. *Dreaming, again.*

"I know you do," I say, and she beams. *Score one for me.* "You rocked that tournament. Rowan will be gone soon enough. Guys like that get bored with towns like this."

I don't tell her about our plan. If it works, Rowan's last stop will be a one-way return ticket to Morgan's.

"May we be so lucky," she says, and her eyes sparkle with mischief. A dimple dots her cheek.

This woman makes me want to get on my knees and do her bidding. Lay my life story before her and ask for mercy only she can provide. *Don't blow it. Give her space.* "You don't need luck," I say. "I listened."

"You did," she says, and the dimple reappears. "Thanks."

"For the escort service?"

"No," she says. "For the company." She unlocks the front door and disappears inside.

In a daze, I stuff my hands in my pockets and shuffle back toward the bar. As my feet cross the scraggly winter grass, I rehash the night and its cosmic timing. Threads tie together in a single moment, on a person taking a chance. Throwing a dart.

I wait at the crosswalk, whistling. In the brewery, lights are on, window shades open to the night. Out front, a few pickup trucks and a familiar navy sedan occupy street side parking spaces. Neon graffiti covers the walls indoors and out. A few customers surround a foosball table while others occupy barstools, jostling for the attention of the cute server with a low-cut top and a well-stuffed tip jar.

On those stools sit Rowan and his cronies.

Before I can talk myself out of sheer idiocy, I fling the door open and stalk to the register. Rowan doesn't see me. He's too busy rehashing how he is the real winner of the contest. His buddies assure him he's right and their talk dissolves into a verbal circle jerk of epic proportions.

The server spots me, smiles, and aims her cleavage my way. She's barely old enough to hand me a beer so I keep my eyes locked on hers.

"I'll take a crowler of your amber," I say, then raise my voice. "Oh, and how about another one of Stay the Fuck out of my Friend's Bar for those three on the end."

The server freezes, her mouth open, trying to compute. I'm

half tempted to give her a kick to reboot the mainframe, but Rowan interrupts me.

"You're like an unwanted stray," he says. "You just don't know when to stay gone."

"My boss is far from a patient man. If I were you, I'd be halfway to LA before he changes his mind about being polite."

"That halfborn?" Rowan snorts. He holds up both hands in mock fear. "Ooh, I'm shaking in my boots."

"I'm going to enjoy wiping that smile off your face."

He moves closer and taps two fingers against my chest. "The only reason you're still standing is because of my good graces. Now do fuck off. You're ruining the party."

He smirks, and I want to deck him. Bad. "I'll make this clear. Leave, or I'll torch that hot rod of yours and send your body parts home on the bus."

At my words, the remaining customers edge to the door. The server ducks behind the counter and crawls toward the kitchen.

"Touch my car and die," he says in a singsong voice. He changes tactics. "Hey, boys, we should go visit that candle maker. Buy something pretty for the house."

Heat floods my bloodstream and my chest heaves. I crack my knuckles in an attempt to gather some patience. *He's got friends.* "You *will* stay away from her and every other woman in this town."

"Or what? You'll hunt me down? I don't think you can keep up."

He snaps his fingers, and two massive wings unfurl from behind his shoulder blades. The enormous, feathered appendages snap outward, like flags in the wind. Black shafts split the pale feathers in stark contrast. His friends follow suit, their wings spread in unison.

Frantic, I look at the other customers. They sit silent, frozen in terror. Mouths open, some with phones in hand, preparing to record. Whatever Rowan did locked them in a moment of fear.

"Get out," Rowan says. "Before I paint this place with their blood."

"You'll regret this," I say, my voice hoarse. The air in the room presses at my lungs.

"Regret isn't part of my vocabulary." Rowan turns his back to me, making a show of taking his seat, wings brushing the ground. He tosses another comment over his shoulder. "Oh, and tell your boss that I'll be staying until I find what I came for."

I look from the winged beasts to the innocent people, frozen in place. I'd be lying to say I'm not tempted to go for his throat, throw caution to the wind. Tonight, however, I will live to fight another day. I take my beer, plunk the money on the counter for when they unfreeze the poor woman, and head for the door.

When the door closes behind me, I turn to witness Rowan's next snap. At once, their wings retract. The customers who were standing stumble, confused. Those seated rub their heads, foggy, while others look around. Rowan sneers at me through the window before returning to his drink.

Outside, I waste no time in calling Ansel. Frost bites at the edges of my coat collar. The moon, a half crescent, pierces Orion's side in the southern sky.

Ansel picks up, the sounds of a boisterous bar in the background. "Yeah?"

"Tell me you've got a Plan B."

CHAPTER

NINE

LOTTE

S unrise stretches out before me, a soft entry to the day. Pink and amber rays touch the mountains, spreading potential across the landscape.

Clouds buck over the hills and make their way across the valley, jostling each other for placement in the baby blue sky as the sun finds its way over the horizon.

I'd wanted time to myself, needed a chance to quell the panic that urged me to run, to start over once again. New town, new business, new people. *Again.*

As I step onto the footpath lined with stones, I give in to the constant push-pull of an existence like mine. I wanted people, needed them to enrich my life. But then their proximity shifts my ability to remain neutral—and everyone pays for that.

This labyrinth, an accidental discovery on one of my runs, winds and doubles back within itself, a mirror to the thoughts wrapping a tight knot around my heart. Like a cobra around a treasure.

I meander my way toward the center, one foot in front of the other. Morning songbirds flit among the trees, ushering in the dawn.

Is this the way of things, the means of protection? Risk aversion by a slew of declined invitations, avoidance of familiarity, and a hermitage that was undesired, but necessary. No one in my life but me?

At the center of the labyrinth, I kneel to set a pinecone among the offerings left by others. Conifers are my favorites. The evergreens promise a steadfast presence that defies winter. On my best of days, that's how I see myself.

I follow the twists and turns back out to take in my favorite city view. This early, the streetlights emit a soft glow, fading out with the coming dawn.

Then, he is behind me. The heavy, silent heat of his breath brushes my neck. The instantaneous awareness of him, inches from me, lights a fire across my skin.

"Good morning."

"It is," he says. "Now."

"Not one for sleeping in?"

He steps to my side, and we stand parallel, looking out across the city. "Some nights I sleep more than others," he says. "And anyway, if it's cool with you, spending sunrise with a woman who smells like creosote after the rain is worth a sleepless night."

"I wouldn't know," I say, forcing back a smile. "But I'll take your word for it."

I'm glad he's here. I spent my evening tossing and turning, debating the choices in front of me and coming up with exactly zero solutions. If I couldn't have answers yet, I could at least enjoy the interim.

I peek at his face. The rays of dawn caress his features and give his skin a golden glow. He frowns a little, as though debating whether to speak. He crosses his arms, biceps bulging in his jacket. With a faraway gaze, he shifts his stance before talking.

"I didn't ask what you are. I figure that's your business," he says to the rising sun. "Last night, though, I second-guessed myself." He looks at me then, an open expression. Curiosity and longing trade places in his expression.

I bristle and look away. *Definitely not what I thought he'd say.* I face the valley again. "Then we've got a mutual problem."

"That we do," he says and sighs. He slides a backpack strap down one arm, flips the pack in front of his body, and extracts a thermos and two metal cups. "Coffee? I don't have anything to put in it, if you're one of those types. But it's decent—and strong enough."

I smile, unable to hold back. *Always surprises, this one.* He pours and I accept a cup. One sip and I nod. "It's good." The liquid warmth floods my chest. "Any chance I can station you at the end of all my hikes?"

He shrugs, then takes a sip from his own mug. "I'd consider volunteering," he says over the rim of his cup.

This man, this place, this moment. I fight the urge to close the gap between us, to crawl inside that jacket, press myself against him, and run my hands all over his body. Tell him everything. *Show* him everything. Wrap ourselves in time and space until all there is to know lays bare between us.

Shut up, brain.

"Truth time. I came up here with ulterior motives."

Fantasy over. "Oh?"

"I've been told you know more than the average candle maker," he begins.

"By whom? Know what?"

He deflects my question with one of his own. "Are you willing to help us?" He pauses, then meets my gaze. "Me."

There is a playful glint in his eyes. An offer to interpret that question in as many ways as I want. Need. Business or pleasure? *Get a damn grip, Lotte.*

It isn't as though I can afford pleasure.

"If you're talking about the Fallen," I begin, resigned to business, "I'll have to think about it."

"Ansel said you'd say that. That you know who—what—they are." He turns back to the sunrise, disappointment creasing his brow. The orb is almost free of its nightly confines, golden along the horizon. "I'll split my fee. Or how about, name your price. I'll figure it out."

I look away and tip the last of the liquid down my throat, making a decision. Tomorrow I can start anew, withdraw. Today, I'll help. Not too much, but enough to rid mortals of another that has no business here. I've gone down this road this far, might as well see it through. "No need," I say, handing him my cup. "Getting rid of those assholes will be my community service."

Joaquin tosses the last of his own coffee back and returns our makeshift picnic to his pack. "We aren't alone. There are others who will help," he says. "I'll set up a meeting spot."

"Consider me ready."

The bag back on his shoulder, he faces me again. The frown of indecision returns. "Being out here alone is a risk."

My fingers twitch as I consider his words. I'd thought the same. Then again, I'd half hoped to run into those ethereal nightmares. No witnesses, no accidental consequences.

I don't say any of this. Instead, I put a hand on his sleeve before he can turn to leave. "Life is a risk. There are more terrors, more haunting things in this world than anyone should have to face. Every day holds the potential for loss of soul, mind, or body as time marches on. Dealing with the unknown, facing it down, is an expectation for those like us."

"Still, it isn't as though we must bear it all ourselves," he says with a small smile. He turns to go, his footsteps silent on the sand.

"Out of curiosity," I call, "what is the assignment—contain or destroy?"

He turns back, a glint in his eyes. "Contain," he says. "Long enough to relish in the destruction."

I turn back to the horizon and nod at the way of the world in front of me. "It's going to be a good day, I can tell."

CHAPTER

TEN

JOAQUIN

We roll up to one of those rent-a-mansions nestled along a golf course in the west hills. By we, I mean myself, Grace, Yanric, and Lotte. And by roll up, I mean we swiped golf carts from the clubhouse and took the back way over the greens.

This is two in the morning in a neighborhood in which homeowners are savvy enough to have made and kept their money or are renting to appear that way. Our targets are of the second variety.

Last night, Yanric volunteered to trail our targets. After popping their wings and threatening to take out the brewery, they'd retreated to this sprawling house among the landscaped yards and winding driveways.

Twenty-four hours later, we snake our way up the hillside to our target, sticking to the shadows.

Two stories at one end, split-level at the other, this is no cottage. From the thirteenth tee box, we see a marble fountain, outdoor ceiling fans, and a wraparound driveway in which sits one dark blue, luxury sedan.

A sprinkle of lights at neighboring houses cast little glow across the grass. We crouch below the retaining wall in the cover of darkness.

"Wow," Grace breathes, taking in the opulent home.

I sneak a glance at Lotte. She wears a skin-tight cat suit with a black beanie pulled low over her hair and black gloves. I can't keep my eyes off the woman.

When she crouches behind a tree, it takes every ounce of gentleman-like calm I can fake not to slide up behind her, wrap my hands around that slick fabric, and run kisses down her neck. I shift my stance to ease the inconvenient distraction below my belt.

I reach down to adjust myself at the exact moment she looks my way. She smirks and I cringe. *Busted.* These creeps have gone after her twice, and here I am objectifying that banging body. *Down, boy.*

I think of laundry day and oil changes, my abuela and the tiny town where I grew up. Taxes and cold showers. Anything to soften the raging heat emanating from my crotch.

Don't look at her. I look at her. *Dammit.*

Curves and black, tumble and bedsheets.

I emit a low growl. Grace shoots me a look, and I point two fingers to signal my move to check out the yard. I need some space to refocus. The others wait.

Chlorine from the bubbling hot tub fills my nostrils as I draw closer. From behind the tub, I hook one black-clad leg over the wall, then follow over with the rest of my body. I land in a low crouch and freeze, listening.

Silence. My pupils dilate into what my mother always called Night Mode. I used to love sneaking around the house, trying to catch her unaware. It was all fun and games until she dropped an entire plate of brownies and my butt was sore for a week. Lesson learned.

Darkness is still my specialty. I ease around the tub to peer in the living room windows, one millimeter at a time.

Nothing. *Nothing?* The inside of the house is void of occupants.

I risk a better view. The owners went for the minimalist look: gray leather couch complete with a half dozen throw pillows in various shades of beige, a chair, a glass coffee table, and a gigantic television. Through the glass, I see into the kitchen. Stainless steel and black. Empty.

I drop back and make my way to the wall. I wave my fingers in a quick gesture and watch as they crawl over the wall. Lotte is all feline, graceful and smooth in her decent. Perfection.

In my periphery, there's a movement in the bushes. I scent grass and fur, with no small amount of fear. With one guttural noise from my throat, I send the deer packing. We don't want witnesses, four-legged or otherwise.

I join my companions at the back of the patio and point at the windows. They follow me. Grace scans for cameras. She taps my hip to point at one anchored in the apex of the roof. We skirt its range.

Around the back of the house, the landscaping makes for tricky footwork. Cacti require nimble navigation. A barrel, the large, round variety with fish hooks for spines, snags the corner of Yanric's pant leg. Lotte helps him disengage, her movement a deft snip of the sharp spine with her fingers.

Reunited, I send Grace and Yanric to fan out on either side. Keeping Lotte with me is a selfish move.

We pause below the sill of a large window. Soft voices come from within. I hold a finger to my lips, a needless yet habitual gesture. Lotte purses her lips. I shrug in apology.

I lift my chin just enough to peek into the room. On the screen is that Jimmy Stewart Christmas movie. Odd choice. It's the one where he almost ends it all in the river, but not before that old guy jumps first to teach him how much the town loves him and his daughter jingles that little bell.

I pop my head up and scan the room. Master bedroom. Heavy dresser, painting of a ship on a stormy sea, massive, four-poster bed. On the dark gray duvet cover is a single feather, silvery in the moonlight.

The others return, offering silent shakes of their heads. The place is empty.

I consider a retreat. We can return to the golf course and reconvene among the trees. I lift my hand to gesture toward the green when I hear Grace's sharp intake of breath at my side.

Black-and-white images cast shadows on the dark wood, but nothing else moves. Grace grabs at the sleeve of my jacket and I follow her stare.

On the dark, polished surface of the dresser sits a mug printed with *Second Shot*, a feather sticking up from inside. My blood runs cold.

We run.

~

THE CAFÉ IS TRASHED. Chairs are strewn about the floor, many with legs broken and splintered. Cups lay shattered on the tile, pieces of the logo winking up at us. The bucket of spent grounds is spilled across the floor, an ocean of dark grains. Grace's cash register yawns open, coins all that's left of the contents. The computer screen is smashed alongside the glass frames holding her business license and first dollar bill.

Grace presses her knuckles to her face in silent horror. The rest of us tiptoe around the debris, checking for clues. Lotte reaches to draw Grace into an embrace. Yanric calls the police.

"They're on their way," he says, and stoops to take pictures of the wreckage. "Assholes. How did they know?"

Grace weeps and sinks to her knees. Lotte fills the last unbroken cup with water and presses it into Grace's hands.

"They came in for coffee this morning," Grace says, her voice wavering. "I told them I don't serve sore losers. When they left without saying anything else, I...doesn't matter now." She presses her palms to her eyes.

We stay quiet until the officer arrives and does a whole lot of not much. He takes his own pictures and promises Grace he'll be in contact. When he leaves, I let the rage settle in.

Grace heads for the storage room for a box of tissues, and Lotte crosses to me to whisper in my ear. "Why her? I thought they'd come after me."

She'd seen what I'd seen. In the middle of the coffee grounds, in stark contrast, a single feather with a black shaft.

In response, I clench my teeth, eager for retribution. "I'm going out. None of you leave here alone," I order, not caring how it sounds.

The door slams behind me, and glass rains down on the sidewalk. I'll come back later, nail up plywood over the ruined door and windows. At the moment, I need release.

Up the block and around the corner, I walk, my focus ahead as I channel anger through my veins.

At the door of the brewery, the same server sees me through the window, fury lighting my features. She hits the floor. I kick open the door. It swings wide and smacks the wall behind.

On a vinyl-topped stool sits one of Rowan's crew. He startles when he sees me, beer spluttering from his lips. He backs off the stool to stand, spilled stout staining his shirt.

My abuela said I'd been a force to be reckoned with since my first big protest at age four. My mother had engaged in an epic battle to wrestle me into a godsawful Sunday suit. That thing was horrid. Too-tight collar, fake pockets, buttons all over, and shoes that pinched my toes. The damn thing was a white and blue nightmare.

I'd thrown a fit on the kitchen floor. My mother threatened me with the wrath of all the saints if I didn't become her sweet *mijo* once more. Abuela said the tiny crease between my black eyebrows deepened, and my cheeks puffed out as I screwed my little face up into the darkest pout I could muster, crossing still-chubby arms over my button-covered chest. When my mother tipped her face to the ceiling to pray for a boy who would listen, I shot out the screen door and into the back yard. She chased behind, but I was faster, determined.

Before she could catch me, I'd covered myself in mud from head to toe. I paid for my actions with no dinner, the loss of my favorite dump truck, and a dozen Hail Marys and four Our Fathers the following Sunday. I remembered sitting on my mother's lap in the confessional while I repeated the words after her, stumbling over their gravity. She shunned me for over a week, so affronted by my behavior. But in the end, the dreaded outfit went in the scrap bin.

This, too, would be worth it.

Two long strides and I stand in front of him. He looks over my shoulder and then to the employee cowering on the floor.

"It won't make a difference," I say.

"What do you want?" he sputters, buying time. He scans my body for weapons, an opening, hope. "I'm just having a beer."

A couple sitting next to him shifts down a few seats. The woman lifts her phone as though to film. I snatch it from her hand and toss it behind the bar. Rash, sure, but I'm all reactive at this point.

"I see the beer," I say. "I'm here about the coffee."

He flinches. "I didn't..."

"You did." I smile and know my pupils have gone dark. *Good.* I want him to read the hatred on my face. I slip my hand into my pocket and lace my fingers under the loop of the iron door knocker I lifted from the cafe. "This is what happens when you touch things that don't belong to you."

I swing a deep uppercut. Bones crack. I take advantage of his stunned recoil to wrap my arm around his neck, pressing the knocker into his shoulder. Flesh sizzles as I drag him out onto the street.

I did my homework.

ELEVEN

T sweep a few piles before Grace takes the broom from my hands.

"I appreciate it," she says. "But the more pathetic it looks for insurance, the better. At least they made it *look* like a regular break-in."

The lights flicker and hum, then turn on. Yanric comes in from the back hall. "I was able to splice some wires back together. Definitely have a pro out to check my work."

I turn to Grace, who hugs the broom handle and stares at the mess. "What can I do to help?"

"Besides rid the world of assholes?" She brings a hand to her forehead and rubs it. "I need a bottle of wine and a bag of pretzels. And bed. I've got a Pomeranian who makes a perfect pillow for crying into—so long as I ply him with treats."

"I'll help you close up," Yanric says. "If Joaquin isn't back by then, Lotte, I'll take you home."

"I can walk myself. It's just a block." Before Yanric protest, I continue, "Joaquin can be mad at me. I can handle it." I scribble my phone number down for both of them, give Grace's arm a squeeze, and with a small, reluctant wave, head out the broken door.

Guilt follows me down the block to my shop. I'd been told

to stay put, but no one, no matter how powerful and sexy, will determine my fate.

I look both ways as I cross each street, an ironic tick. Mica in the cement sparkles in the sidewalks under the street lamps. Within three minutes, I'm in my own shop and bolt the lock behind me.

I won't sleep tonight. My brain, a pile of human-induced mush, needs mindless activity in which it can decompress. I turn off the shop lights and head for the workroom.

Cabinets and shelving stripe each wall above the counter-tops. In the center of the space is a massive butcher block island with various drawers to hold waxes, oils, and all manner of natural dyes and fragrances. Here, I'm an artist.

Though you wouldn't know from the calendar, spring is closer than most realize. In the fall, I pour jars that will comfort, warm, and enrich a home through the holidays. This time of year, I make candles to call the light back, to welcome and encourage what is new.

I've learned from watching others to complain when I see Christmas decorations in October, to whine when red and pink takes over before Yule is half complete. Humans love to bemoan greed cloaked in holiday cheer yet paint their winters with every opportunity for festivity. This is why ancestors lined the winter months with celebrations. When darkness falls, the smallest pinprick of light pulls us forward to the spring.

I don my tool apron, then flip the switch on my wax melter and drag a stool to the island. With a sharp pair of shears, I cut cord lengths. I knot one end of each strand under a wick tab and tie a small glass bead to the top. With a dozen prepared wicks in hand, I rummage in my essential oils for the right bottles. Grapefruit, lemon, lavender, and sage bring spring to mind. Maybe some lemongrass. I lose myself in planning my mixtures.

When first on my own, money was tough to materialize. I considered hairstyling, but there's too much intimacy. Too many questions I wouldn't be able to answer. Textiles seemed too obvious, and fashion is a frustrating distraction. My skill set is more limited than most would guess, but I needed something.

In the end, I became my own boss. This way, I dabble in my passion, marking time with beeswax and bergamot, all while creating something beautiful for someone's home. No one has a false sense of control over me, and I can keep a careful distance between myself and customers. Candle making is soothing and solitary.

It wasn't until I'd stumbled into a candle shop in Albuquerque that I fell in love with the craft. The owner was kind, instructive. Within a week, I had a business plan and a place to stay should I ever come through again.

Prescott, a pit stop on my way across the country, called to me. Sure, I knew what was there, what called to those from the otherworld. But for me, it was the charm of an old west town. The farmers' market and the bistro with heavenly pasta. The painted hills and endless hiking trails. Its history—the people.

I remove a set of jars and line them on the counter. After scent, color, and a careful stir, I ladle the liquid wax into the vessels. As I pour, I run through recent events, turning them over in my mind in search of insight.

There was the contest, the confrontation, and the stakeout. My role in the whole big string of events. Had I snuggled up in my window seat instead of throwing darts, I'd be blissful, ignorant.

I'd also be missing the most exciting things to happen in my life for months. *Years.*

We wear our roles like winter coats, sometimes. So accustomed to their weight, we forget to take them off. I'd practiced staying out of the picture for so long.

In that phase, I'd never met someone like Joaquin. Diving headfirst into the messy, changing present moment is exhilarating. Thrilling. *Freeing.*

For someone to notice me, appreciate me, and want me to be a part of their world is new and exciting. My life holds a spark now. Rather than smother it, I want nothing more than to fan the flames and watch it grow. So much for my planned retreat.

Then, I remember the threats, the feathers, the break in. Was I truly a helper or only spurring the situation toward an inevitable, disastrous conclusion? Was my involvement only beneficial to my own selfishness?

A shattering from within the shop breaks my concentration. I stop my work, listening. Stillness. I squint toward the door. I locked myself in, didn't I?

"Hello? We're closed," I say from within the workroom, willing calm to meter my speech. It can't be anyone. Has to be no one.

Another crash.

I storm to the door and push it open.

Two figures stand in the middle of my shop. Each holds a candle, their faces lit by the light spilling in from the workroom doorway.

Wings spread, one holds Front Porch Lemonade, and the other brandishes Baker's Dream. They look like actors in one of those cheesy aromatherapy commercials. I can't help but snicker.

"That's a new one," says Rowan. "Most people with any sense cower before me. Only a pureborn fool would laugh."

I ignore him and turn to his companion. He has a length of rope looped over one shoulder, out of place with cargo pants and a preppy sweater. "Cinnamon and vanilla? I wouldn't have pegged you for a Midwestern housewife," I say, apologizing internally to all the women who fit that bill. Stereotypes are a bitch. I shrug at the guy, dismissive. "But I guess it fits."

He holds the label close to his face to read as I make my way toward them.

"See the sign?" I point, a distraction. "I have rights in this town, and right now I'm refusing to serve you. Get out." I maintain eye contact to allow for one hand to slip into my apron pocket, unnoticed. "Do you need me to spell it out? Type 'Home' into your GPS? Oh wait, you're no longer welcome there."

"Touch my car, and I'll make sure it's the last thing you do."

Rowan drops the candle he holds and shards spray outward. I do my best not to flinch and spot a trickle of blood on my forearm. Earlier I'd rolled up my sleeves in the workroom, not planning to encounter splintering glass.

"That ego mobile? You couldn't pay me to ride shotgun in that embarrassment."

"Don't pretend for one minute that you are in any way better than we are," Rowan says, his voice deepening as he picks up another candle.

"Did you not hear me? Leave."

Rowan takes a few steps my way, holding the candle. "How many towns have you inhabited then left? Lovers whose beds you've left empty?" He crosses his arms and appraises me with steely gray eyes. "Men who wake up to cold sheets and a wet dream. That's all you are to anyone, and all you'll ever be."

There's a roaring in my ears and my chest heaves. "You have fifteen seconds to get out of my shop before I call the police."

Like a whip, his hand flies back and flings the candle at the wall by my head. The glass explodes, spraying the room. "You and I both know the law is pointless."

He pauses at a table and pushes each candle to the floor, one by one, in a cascade of ruin. His boots crunch over the detritus as he moves closer.

Rowan stops inches from my face. He reaches for my chin and holds it between his thumb and forefinger. "Look at you, so pretty. Such a waste. What I wouldn't give to..." He smiles. "Maybe I will. As I'm sure you like to say, there's no time like the present." He turns to his partner. "Should we have a little fun and games? Nothing I enjoy more than a true test of power."

But Rowan's friend isn't listening. His eyes are on the street, squinting at two figures making their way across the square.

I freeze, like a rabbit in the snow, the coin toss of fight-or-flight spinning in my mind. My hand curls into a fist, finger-tips searing my palm.

"You see," Rowan says. "I have friends. Compatriots. You have no one. And the saddest part? The only one to blame for that—is you."

Fight.

Rowan's friend calls, "Hey, that mutt has Valir!" He spins and runs for the door.

I launch over the counter and before Rowan can escape, jam my scissors deep into his neck.

His hands fly to the handle as he makes a gurgling noise and stumbles toward the door and out into the night.

Shaking, I dial the one person who can help.

A woman picks up, loud music muffling her words. "I need to speak with your boss," I shout.

While I wait, a scene plays out through the shop window.

The trio is reunited when an injured Rowan and his buddy attack Joaquin who releases the one they called Valir. Within seconds, Joaquin is on the ground, and they've tied him up with the rope intended for me. They hoist him upward and drag him down an alleyway.

The voice I've been desperate to hear comes to the phone. "Yeah?"

"They've got him."

TWELVE

JOAQUIN

When getting your ass kicked, it's not the time to lose focus.

But here I am, distracted.

To be fair, I started this with the upper hand. Pure adrenaline brought that winged abomination to his knees. A rusty iron door knocker kept him there.

I'd hauled him out of that dinky dive and into the plaza. At that time of night there are few people around–and no one lingers among the trees. The reject knew better than to protest. He knows and I know that were humans to get involved, he'd be locked up and studied while I'd be heralded. He gets dissected and preserved in formaldehyde as the masses claim miracles really do exist. I go back to what I do best–taking out his brethren.

In my initial success, I failed to consider the proximity of said brothers. Three of them, one of me.

Next thing I know, I'm on the ground, spitting mad. Two hold me while one kicks me in the gut until I can't see straight. The predator became the prey.

People wonder why if the things that go bump in the night are real, they aren't seen. Witnessed. Those same people often openly exploit, murder, and otherwise harm their known, living world without mercy.

Who would want to be seen by a species so lethal to everything, including itself?

I'm an on-the-fringes type of guy, regardless. Abuela always said, if there's a center of the party, I'll be farthest from that point. She was right, and that's why I, and not my abuela or anyone else in my family, am alive today. But that story is for another time.

What rankles me is that I'd had him. I'd been so close to delivering him to the boss, job well done. I'd wielded that hunk of iron like a champ.

As my head spins with pain, I attempt to focus on the stars above. Heavenly bodies wink at me as I lie on the cold ground, blood oozing from my nose, a rib or two out of place. Tiny moth holes in a blackened blanket.

The lifetime of a star depends on its mass—learned that in high school. Iron is their kryptonite, too, its atomic weight too much to sustain. Some stars will shift through phases until they peter out as a forgotten white dwarf. Others swell in mass, collapsing upon themselves before exploding in a catastrophic supernova. Iron is their undoing, the beginning of their end.

Everything in this universe is finite, myself included. As I watch the tiny sparkles, gargantuan in reality, minuscule in appearance, I remember my old astronomy teacher. Mr. Saab said that in the vastness of space and time, nothing small matters.

In the grand scheme of things, I don't matter. If these are my last moments on this planet, in this galaxy, I'll keep my eyes on the stars. For in our beginnings will we find peace in our end.

"Why is he smiling like that? The prick."

I can't imagine what I look like, but I know how I feel. I shift one swollen eye to take in my captors.

Rowan, or at least I think it's him—my vision is swimming —yanks a pair of scissors from his neck. Instead of blood, a black, viscous liquid oozes from the nasty wound. I grimace and give my head a shake to check if I'm hallucinating.

Freed, my former prisoner kicks me again in the ribs. I groan. "That is for ruining a perfectly good night." He lifts a foot, bringing his ridiculous pair of brand new snakeskin boots into view, and brings it down to crunch the fingers on my right hand. "And that is for the door knocker."

I wince and attempt to roll over and cradle my hand, but my ribs will not comply. My focus swims in and out of view. They drag me across the square, down the alley, and into the atrium. The stucco walls glow navy in the moonlight. From between the tree branches, Orion watches.

When not held captive by three celestial train wrecks, I spend night after night studying the sky. As a boy I'd climb out on our rooftop and try to count them, giddy at the impossible task. Grown Joaquin knows most of the constellations by heart. I list Orion's stars in my head to keep myself from passing out. *Rigel, Betelgeuse, Bellatrix, Saiph...*

Rowan grabs a shock of my hair and lifts my head. I wince, squinting at him with one eye.

"What's the matter—are we hurting you?"

"No," I whisper between shallow breaths. I screw up my face with the muscles able to take part. "Yuck. Your breath reeks like my uncle's armpit. Heard of a toothbrush?" *Apologies, Tío.*

Rowan roars in frustration and slams my head against the ground. "Listen, mongrel. You tell me where to find the weir, and I'll consider leaving your girlfriend in one piece."

"Girlfriend—who? That's news to me."

"You know who I mean. That hot number with the coffee shop."

I snort-laugh, causing snot to blow out one nostril in a bubble. "She's got a girlfriend."

"Got a...what?" Confusion sweeps his face, and he releases his hold on my scalp.

"As in, she dates women, you feathered troglodyte. Catch up with the twenty-first century."

He shakes his head as though dodging the new facts.

"Never mind that. I'll destroy her and every other human you love."

"Too late," I say, a mixture of blood and saliva trickling from my lips and down to my collar. I love this shirt. Going to need a new one if I live through this.

"What?"

From my crumpled position, I take stock. I consider if any of my limbs will function long enough to get me out of the alley. Planning causes my building headache to throb more, so I focus my gaze on the tree tops. Each branch is a traceable extension off the wizened trunk. It may have been the starlight, or the addled state of my brain, but I'd later swear to have seen silver threads winding through the woodgrain.

"Someone beat you to that," I say, my eyes on the tree. "You'll have to come up with another threat."

"What the...? Enough!" He punches me in the jaw, and my teeth clip my tongue. "Tell me where we can find the weir. I know it's inside this building, and I'm getting godsdamn sick of waiting."

"Maybe you should speak to the manager."

I've never been more grateful to hear someone's voice.

I can't see Ansel from my prone spot on the cobblestones, but I can picture the guy. He's got the look of a Viking who swallowed Brad Pitt. Piercing blue eyes that turn gray when he's ticked off. Shoulder-length, dirty brown hair. I told him to quit with the man bun, but since he doesn't give a damn about luring ladies, he ignores my fashion tips. Jeans and a work shirt, collar buttoned, even in summer. He tells the curious it's so his neck doesn't get cold, but I know the truth. Once, a flirty customer hooked her finger in his neckband and gave a playful tug. That was the one and only time I'd witnessed him lay hands on a woman. He grabbed her wrist in a lightning reflex, and I swear his eyes glowed silver fire in warning. Haven't seen that groupie since.

"Take us there, halfborn, and I'll consider returning him to you in fewer pieces."

Ansel ignores Rowan and calls to me. "Fairly certain I'm not paying you to take a nap."

"Sorry, boss, I was taking out the trash here and..."

Rowan bellows into the night. "Is every godsdamn Earthbound a comedian?"

"Definitely not. You have yet to land a joke of any type," I say, spitting blood from between my teeth. "Even my brick house of an employer over there will crack a smile every other Sunday. I even heard him make fun of his granny. Once."

"I did not."

"You did. You said her coffee was so strong it would put hair—"

"Stop!"

The ground shakes. From my crumpled position, I see flames lick out from the soles of Rowan's shoes. There is the sound of metal unsheathed and a sharpness at my throat.

"One more word, and my wrist slips," Rowan says. "Take me to the weir. Now."

"Someone mention beer?"

Four heads whip around to scout out the unfamiliar voice. Or at least this is what I picture in my head because if my vertebrae hadn't been screaming, I would've been the fifth.

"I prefer wine with my charcuterie, but I'll take a beer with the right pairing."

"Who in Nether are you?"

"Get back inside, old man," Ansel says. "This isn't your fight."

"Listen to the halfborn," Rowan warns. "The time of wielding wands has come and gone. There's a new power coming, and it doesn't play with sticks."

In a heartbeat, the pressure is gone from my neck.

"Can't prep the cheese plate without the proper tools."

"A metal mage," one of the winged breaths.

Hollis chuckles. I bet he's holding the knife that was once at my throat.

"Please," he says. "I'm just a shopkeeper who appreciates a good tool. Reminds me of my gardening knife. Picked that up in Tokyo. It's perfect for weeding out the unwanted." He pauses—I assume to examine the knife now in his hand. "This one is much nicer. Fancy. Can't say I'm a fan of bone handles, though, being vegan, and all. I'll make an exception for antiquity, I suppose. Perfect timing, too, since I was just about to settle in with a wedge of havarti. I'd extend an invitation, but this isn't my crowd."

Rowan's boots fly over my head as he lunges for where Hollis must be standing. He lands with a thud. There's a crash of trash cans and everyone is yelling. A body slams against the fire escape.

Hollis races around me and comes into view. He mutters a string of words, his eyes on the window box across the atrium. A tendril of a vine whips toward us, brushing my cheek. There is a yelp as Valir hits the ground and is dragged past me by the vine. Another vine shoots overhead. I use what strength I have to bicycle my legs against the ground until I'm facing the fight.

Valir dangles overhead, the vine suspending him from the fire escape. Ansel grabs for for the other one, and wrestles him to the ground. Rowan dodges the second vine and lunges for Hollis. I try to yell out but choke on my words. There is a soft sound like the slicing of a ripe peach. Hollis slides to the ground, a pair of scissors in his side.

"No," I cry, in shock. My muted protest goes unheard as the light drains from Hollis's face.

Behind Ansel, Iris screams from the back door of the bar. Failinis barks from behind her, a deep woof. A jumble of voices spill out from the doorway.

Rowan yanks the pair of scissors from out of the body and cuts the vine that holds Valir. The two of them flee, footprints echoing against the brick walls.

THIRTEEN

LOTTE

T o say I watch it all as a helpless bystander is a lie.

I see every excruciating moment—and I panic, torn.

This is my weakness: I have the crippling urge to do something, to take a stand. Yet all I do is wait, watch, and allow fate to play out.

When a woman's scream pierces the night, I'm shaken from my stupor in the alleyway. The winged intruders rush past me in a flurry of ice and feathers. Rowan shoves a bloodied pair of scissors at my chest as he races by, laughing.

Mobile again, I run to join those huddled around the two bodies lying on the concrete. One is moaning, the other is still.

Sirens pierce the night. Ansel turns to the bartender. "Iris, keep everyone inside. Make Heidi help you. And for godssake, don't let that dog out."

Whispers and cries are heard from within as Iris jostles the crowd back from the door. Ansel hits his knees to probe Joaquin, who groans. "At least buy me dinner first."

"You aren't going anywhere dressed like that."

"But that bloated albatross said I have a girlfriend."

A girlfriend? I move closer, sliding along the wall. I avoid the crumpled form by the trash cans and keep my eyes on Joaquin.

"News to me. I've got to get you out of here before the uniforms arrive. I'll do my best to be gentle."

"You wouldn't know gentle if it bit you on the ass."

"Now who's got a girlfriend?"

Joaquin snorts. "You made me laugh, and it isn't even Sunday."

Ansel cradles his friend and deadlifts him from the ground. Joaquin is almost as tall as the bar owner but not nearly as broad, yet it makes for an awkward embrace. "These steps and the flight of stairs to the office are all that's between you and as many shots of top-shelf bourbon as you can stomach while we wait for the nurse."

"I'm counting them," Joaquin says. "The steps and the shots."

Ansel starts for the door then turns to me. "You coming?"

"I...uh...I—"

"You won't want to be here in the next two minutes, clutching those and looking like that, or there will be more questions than you want to answer."

I follow him inside.

WHILE ANSEL TALKS with the police, I wait with Joaquin. I can't imagine the story told, but I'm grateful for the Morgan's sweatshirt Ansel tossed my direction before heading downstairs.

Joaquin waits, stretched across Ansel's desk. I hadn't been certain he was conscious, let alone that he knew I was in the room, until he addressed me.

"I should've been nicer to him," he says, his voice a raspy whisper.

"You shouldn't talk. Ansel said a nurse will be here soon to help."

Joaquin's chuckle is a bitter sound. "Some wounds will never mend."

Moments later, Ansel ushers a woman into the room. Tall

and flaxen-haired, fingers manicured in bright pink, she plunks down a vintage doctor's case in one of the wingback chairs and unsnaps the clasp. She withdraws a stethoscope and tucks it into her ears before pressing the small pad to Joaquin's chest.

"Oof, this looks bad." Her voice is the high-pitched sound of a young girl, too sweet to be confronting a mangled body. She bends at the waist, her cleavage on full display. "How about we give our favorite client a once-over and see what we can do, hmm? Been out playing rough again, I see."

If I hadn't been in the office of a pioneer-built, western bar, I would swear Cinderella incarnate had walked through the door. I pace the room, not into watching this fairytale woman pat down the man on the table.

"You ought to give me a punch card at this rate."

"Indeed. Want to tell me about it?"

"There was this huge ogre, and I challenged him to a thumb war. Only his thumb is as big as my thigh and..." He coughs and swears.

"It's all right." She pats his arm in a gentle assurance. "Stories and shots when you are back in beast mode. Shall I?"

I startle when Joaquin looks at me. He smiles with the corner of his mouth and moves his head the slightest degree. "Yes—please."

The woman reaches again into her bag and extracts a vial. She transfers the contents into a hypodermic needle which she then jabs into the flesh of his glute. He bucks once, then a smile spreads across his face and his eyes close. She tucks the empty bottle back into her case and snaps it closed.

At the sound of Joaquin's soft snores, she picks up the bag and turns to me. "Don't worry. He's not my type."

"Excuse me?"

She raises her eyebrows, then looks down at my hands. The tips sparkle like trick birthday candles.

"Even if he were interested in me," she says, not retreating, "I've got my hands full." She brushes past me and heads for the door, the scent of peonies and ether trailing in her wake.

"Wait. I don't... I mean..."

"It's okay," she says, stooping to scratch behind the ears of an enormous dog passed out on a bed in the corner. "Your secret is safe with me." She stands to hand me her card. "If you ever need me—well, not you, personally, of course—I'm a phone call away." She looks at Joaquin and then back to me and smiles, raising both eyebrows. "Good luck with that one."

Ansel opens the door before the nurse can exit the room. "Got rid of the cops," he tells us. "Told them we heard a fight and found Hollis. Couldn't identify the attackers—not local." He gestures to Joaquin. "He going to live?"

"Another day—at least."

"Good," Ansel says. "Thanks."

The woman nods and ducks out. Ansel studies the sleeping Joaquin.

"Stupid. When will you learn the simple math of three against one?"

"More like 2 1/2," I say, and shrug. "He managed to take out the one with a doorknocker." I don't bring up my scissors.

"He is twice as brave as he is idiotic," Ansel says to Joaquin's dozing form. He then turns to me. "Speaking of bravery, thank you for the shield. You bought me time to hide my friend—and wash your scissors."

I wince. "Of course." I hadn't been certain anyone noticed my intervention in the atrium. I now had that answer.

Shields are something I employ to prevent interference. They prevent disruption at key moments in time. My one useful parlor trick.

"I don't know what you're doing here," Ansel says. "And I make it my business to know what everyone is doing here."

I know he isn't talking about humans. "Sounds tiring," I say, attempting to lighten the moment. I don't know what to say to this man. I know too much of him, his origin and his demise, and this is why for me, distance is always the easier option.

"It can be. It can also be useful. I'm hoping in exchange for my discretion, you'll share some information."

I bite my lip. "What kind of information?"

"What do you know about this place?"

Ansel and I stare at each other, weighing our next words with care.

I start. "I know what it is that you guard, what is underneath your bar. I know also what is next door. Their kind has a resistance to fate. I'm not surprised they seek control over that which is not theirs to wield."

"Hollis told me those three are also here for an artifact. A certain item I, too, have been hunting. One that allows certain...travel."

"How did he know?"

"We found a journal," he explains. "What do you know of it?" Ansel watches my face, scrutiny in the lines around his eyes.

I shake my head. "First I've heard of such an object, whatever it may be." I, too, can keep my cards close at hand.

Ansel stares at me a moment. When he decides I speak the truth, he puffs out a breath he'd been holding and runs a hand down his face.

Coughing from the desktop wakes the dog. Failinis gets to his feet, stretches, and then moves over to Joaquin to lick at his hand. "Ew, gross," Joaquin says. "Come on, Fail, I know where that mouth has been." Joaquin lifts his hand and clutches at his chest through another round of coughs. "Godsdamnit." With a grunt, he struggles to sit upright. He wipes the bloody crust from around his mouth with the back of one hand. "Hollis?"

Ansel shakes his head.

Joaquin looks at the ground beneath his dangling feet, then looks up again, solemn. "Permission to wreak havoc?"

"Granted."

Joaquin swings his legs over the side of the desk and stands. He brushes off the front of his jeans and pats down his pockets.

"You're going after them now!? You were comatose two minutes ago."

"No time like the present. Experience tells me the chemicals rushing through my system will propel me through all kinds of reckless decisions in the name of vengeance." He turns to Ansel. "Cops gone?"

"Should be."

"I'll need access to the vault."

"Granted." Ansel shifts, thinking. "Not sure I have any iron bullets, but we can get creative. Or there's always blades."

"My favorite." Joaquin describes the house in the hills as he and Ansel talk logistics.

Impatient, I interrupt. "I'm coming with you."

Both of them frown at me, confusion in their expressions. Ansel opens his mouth to protest, but Joaquin cuts him off. "How fast can you be ready?"

"I'll be back in ten."

TEN MINUTES LATER, I return in head-to-toe black. I pull the balaclava up from around my neck to cover my hair. "I assume we are going by bike?"

Joaquin hands me an iron spike. "Is there another way?"

I examine the weapon, and Ansel says, "Train tracks."

Joaquin slides two fire pokers into an X of straps across his back. "These won't make for the most comfortable ride, so I'll owe you a better one another day. Deal?"

"Deal. I prefer we arrive well armored for this dance."

The ride, a cautious tour of the back streets, isn't as uncomfortable as promised. I grip the outsides of his thighs with the insides of my own and keep my hands on his hips. I tilt my head back to watch the stars.

We can get so used to a thing being there we forget to look for it. Forget to acknowledge its beauty, the marvel that is the Milky Way, a wash of cosmic detritus in the night sky.

Tonight, on the back of a motorcycle driven by a man who makes me feel things I hadn't known were possible, I feel small and grateful. I feel human.

Joaquin cuts the engine as we reach the outskirts of the neighborhood. We make our way along the golf course greens and up to the house.

This time, all lights are blazing. Heavy bass thumps through the windows, a tangible vibration. From our vantage point among the boulders, we see our duo and some women, too. Rowan grinds against two of them, moving to the beat. The third woman sits in Valir's lap, stroking his hair while he glowers into the distance.

I whisper into the darkness. "What did Ansel do with their third?"

"Locked him up...for safekeeping."

I scrutinize the group. Ansel mentioned an artifact. I can't see these amateurs in charge of something so important. Still, they have an agenda.

"Do we wait for them to go to sleep or just for the girls to leave?" Joaquin asks at my ear, sending a shiver down my spine. "Your preference."

"They don't have it yet," I say.

"Have what?"

"Whatever it was that Hollis sacrificed his life to protect."

Joaquin frowns at the scene in front of us. "It's not like they'd leave anything precious in a rental, anyway."

I inhale a sharp intake of breath, and Joaquin's eyes go wide. "The car," we mouth, a simultaneous realization.

He points to the driveway. We sneak around the side of the house toward the sleek vehicle. He points to me and then toward the house before sliding in the gravel under the car. There is a spark and inside the car, the blinking red light goes out. With a soft click, he opens a passenger door.

I keep watch as shuffles come from within the vehicle as he checks every nook and cranny. A silent shadow flaps overhead as an owl lands in a nearby tree—our only witness.

"Bingo." His affirmation floats into the night.

Minutes later, Joaquin is out of the car. We retrace our steps to the bike. The ritzy neighborhood falls away in the background.

At the crest of a hill, he slows and parks the bike behind a copse of trees. We hike a quarter mile to another hilltop.

Dawn inches over the horizon. He takes a seat on a rocky outcrop facing east and pats the spot next to him. I join the watch.

As the sun peeks over the mountains, he reaches into a pocket of his jacket and extracts a stone dangling from a gold chain. It glints in the faint light. The stone itself is pale. I stare, disbelieving.

"Found it hanging from the rearview mirror," he says.

"That's one place to keep a priceless artifact."

"Reckon we have time to finish watching the sunrise before they come after it?"

"I do," I say, and lean my shoulder against his.

FOURTEEN

JOAQUIN

There's nothing like the bottom of a glass for reflecting the worst of your recent decisions.

I roll the cut lowball along its edge across the counter. The crystal facets catch the light as I stare at the many sides of myself.

Lotte's words have not left me. Have I been wasting away in my bitterness?

Ansel is tied up with the produce vendor, and I have time to kill. Iris sets a second drink next to my empty glass.

"Thanks, greenhorn." I reach for my back pocket.

"Compliments of the owner."

"A decent guy."

"Easy on the eyes, that's for sure," Iris says. She walks away, then stops and comes back. "I've heard about you. Don't let that luck run out."

Iris moves off to the next customers. Word of Hollis made the rounds, and the bar is quieter tonight, subdued. Ansel said in some ways it makes reconnaissance easier—though it can't be good for tips. In another month, Whiskey Row will bustle again, the tragic death old news.

With a sip, the peaty scent of Scottish bogs fills my nostrils once again. Lotte is nowhere to be seen. Safer that way.

Ansel, fresh from negotiations, pours himself a matching scotch. We clink glasses. There's comfort in a habit like that. Twenty years in and we're an old married couple.

He leans forward, holding his glass in front of his lips while he speaks. Ansel has his bar swept for bugging devices every other week but operates as though one can never be too careful.

"Sharon appreciated the report. She's eager to meet our guests," he says, then takes a swig.

I swirl my own amber liquid. "Does she know who sent them the invitation?

"She has screenshots of the journal. She'll investigate. Meanwhile, assume she's interested in meeting them in whatever way, shape, or form can be arranged."

"Did she seem...worried?"

Ansel is quiet. He presses his glass between his palms. "More—surprised. Gave open access to whatever resources we need."

"So, she *is* spooked." I take a sip and let the liquid sit on my tongue a moment before swallowing.

My best friend changes the subject. "When are we going to talk about her?" He stares at the wall of liquor bottles behind the bar, avoiding my gaze.

"Her, who—Lotte?" A couple of decades with someone and they can practically smell your emotions. "She's gorgeous," I say. "Anyone with half a hormone would agree."

"Not her," Ansel says, and looks at me. His forehead creases with concern.

My heart sinks into my stomach, and flashbacks flood my mind. My throat dries, and I come up silent each time I attempt a response.

"You don't owe me any explanation," he continues. "I just didn't want you to miss a real future. Something good, something real. Sometimes we have to let go of the past or we're doomed to drag it behind us. I don't think she would've wanted that for you." He tips the rest of his glass down his throat and steps down from his stool. He claps me on the shoulder and moves off.

I stare at the hardwood surface in front of me. He's right, I know. Yet how can I honor those who came before, be with those in the present, and stay true to myself? The weight of it knots in my chest. I don't know if it's the whisky or the heartache, but my head pounds.

There's a crash as the front door slams open. In the doorway, Rowan and Valir block the exit, their eyes on me. Rowan kicks a barstool, sending it toppling onto the floor.

"Just the man we wanted to see. I'm missing something valuable, and I think you might know where to find it." His eyes glow red, bloodshot.

"Hey, Ansel," I call. "Did you hear a squeak? I'm sure I just heard a mouse or some other irritating pest. Might need to call an exterminator."

In two strides, Rowan is at the bar. He grabs hold of my jacket and drags me off the stool, spilling my glass across the woodgrain. The remaining liquid drips onto the bar seat and then onto the floor. "That was a damn good scotch," I say, brushing at my jacket. "Show some respect."

"I'm not playing around," he says. Rowan holds up two fingers and snaps, freezing the humans around us in place. Those in the bar are as still as wax figures. "Empty your pockets. All of them. If it's not there, I'll check every orifice on your body until I find that amulet."

I reach into my pockets. "Amulet...amulet...nope, don't think I have one of those. Ansel has a lost and found. You could ask him."

Rowan's eyes flash and he grits his teeth. His wings unfurl. The spectacular spread blocks the lights behind him. The blackness of the feather shafts has spread. Each feather is now half gray, half white.

"Doesn't look like you're feeling well," I say, peering over his shoulder. "You should get that checked out. I'd give you the number of my gal, but she has standards, and they don't include assholes."

He yanks my face closer to his. In my periphery, I see a shape move behind the bar. "I will burn this place to the ground, dog. But first, I'll have you watch as I tear that woman, limb from limb."

Ansel steps forward and slams his fist on the bar. "Not in here," he says, his voice a steady warning. "You have ten seconds to get out of my bar. We have rules in this establishment, godsdamnit, and you will follow them or leave." His eyes are the white of lightning.

At this, Rowan drops me, and I gasp gulps of air. He presses his palms together and then slowly spreads them apart. A fireball builds between them, a swirling mass of blue flames at its center that fans outward to a golden rim. With a grin, he throws it over my shoulder. It lodges among the bottles where it burns a hole straight through the woodwork.

"Or what?" Rowan says and crosses his arms.

At this, Ansel's nostrils flare. He reaches for his sword, an assumed relic hung from hooks above his register. He lifts the blade above his head then brings it down on the bar top. The wood splinters, sparks flying. Ansel's body heaves with rage, his eyes a blinding white. He swells, growing by the second.

Rowan stumbles on a table as he backs up, then he and Valir run for the door.

I follow them into the night. On the sidewalk, I leap on Valir's back and swing the fire poker I've carried since our last encounter. It clocks him in the chest, and he falls. I'm on top of him, pinning him with the iron and searing flesh. He hasn't sprouted his wings, and now I know why. At the place between his shoulders where they would have been is nothing but a pair of rotting stumps.

I shudder. "Gross. You should have those looked at." I pull tighter on the bar, and he grimaces. "Where you're going, they don't care how you arrive. Maybe they'll make you a prosthetic."

"Shut up, mutt," he manages to say.

"Make me." I press the bar upward, slamming his jaw shut.

"Don't mind if I do," says Rowan from behind. He grabs me and jerks me off his partner. Valir wheezes puffs of smoke onto the grass.

Rowan throws me to the ground and pins me. One knee on my throat, the other on my gut. He's incredibly strong and I am short on options.

"One more time," he says between heavy breaths. "Amulet. Location." He shifts his knee from my throat to my collarbone, and I gasp from the pain.

"You should really get your buddy checked out," I say. "And maybe stop smoking. It'll ruin your health. Oh wait... That's already happening, isn't it?" His wings have darkened further. Only streaks of white remain on the feathers.

Rowan's eyes go black, and he summons a fireball with his hands. He throws it in the branches of the closest tree. "If I have to destroy this entire town to find that amulet, I will."

"You wouldn't make it," I choke out. "They'll take you out."

Valir, recovered, laughs. "There aren't enough of you to stop what's coming."

"If they are anything like you two, all we'll need is a garden hose."

"You underestimate us, mortal." Valir summons a ball of flames and holds it above his head. "I'm going to enjoy—"

A fire poker pierces his abdomen, cutting him off.

In an instant, he's engulfed in flames. Flashes of gold and blue, then nothing but a pile of ash is left where Lotte stands, poker in hand.

"You bitch!" Rowan releases me and stumbles backward.

"I thought that guy would never shut up."

I give a gentle probe of my neck. "Thank you."

She nods. "Should I call the nurse?" One eyebrow rises and she smiles. "Keri gave me her card."

Sirens pierce the night. There is a flapping sound, and Rowan is gone.

"Fuck," she hisses. We'd both forgotten the other beast. "Can you walk?"

"There's one way to find out." She hauls me up and puts my good arm over her shoulder. We hobble across the street as two sheriff's vehicles roll up near the blazing tree.

"You didn't have to save me," I say. Each step is equal parts pain and pleasure.

"I did," she says. "It's not your time."

FIFTEEN

LOTTE

I intervened. *Killed.* Every other thought is this one.

The reality, this new definition of who I am, what I can become, rankles me to the core.

There will be time to freak out later. For now, I'll stuff it down. That is the future. In the now, I am here with him.

"I owe you."

The nurse has once again come and gone, winking at me as she slipped back into the night. I shrug off the debt. He doesn't know this isn't possible, not in a thousand realms could it be. "You would've done the same."

"Dinner? In thanks."

I blink. Hesitation pulls at me, and I run my tongue along my lower lip.

"You do eat, don't you?" A crack in his lip splits as he smiles, teasing.

"I do—eat." What I don't say is that I've never eaten with a man. On purpose.

"I need to clean up." He gestures to the bloodstains. I don't point out the grass and sticks snarled in his hair. He'll find them. "Pick you up at seven?"

I swallow. "Okay. Yes."

At 6:55, I'm anything but ready.

I try on and dismiss every outfit in my closet. Candlemaker Lotte, Stakeout Lotte, or...On a Date Lotte? I huff in frustration.

The rumble of an engine interrupts my indecision. I cringe in the middle of my bedroom, wearing only my underthings. They won't matter—tonight.

"Godsdamnit," I say, trying on the curse. It doesn't fit— yet.

Two minutes later, I'm out the door.

His eyebrows lift as I accept the helmet. I place it on my head, and he snaps the strap below my chin, a pointed opportunity to draw close. He's inches from my face. "You look fantastic," he breathes.

"Black on black?" I'd slipped into a pair of faux leather pants and a body skimming sweater.

"My favorite."

I don't miss that he scans each street of the intersection before taking off. "Expecting company?" I ask, guessing at his caution.

He glances around one more time. "Hope not. I've never been one to share a date."

He pops the kickstand, and we are off.

Date, then.

The miles breeze by as we head out of town and into the valley. The cold whips against my cheeks, and my hair flies back from my face. Nothing between us but the night, I lean into Joaquin. The muscles in his back shift as we take the turns. A sliver of the moon lifts into the sky. I savor the moment, this man, and the night.

At a rundown strip mall in Prescott Valley, he eases the bike to a stop in front of a hole-in-the-wall restaurant.

"Anzalone's. Never heard of this place."

"I've known the family for years," he says. "The cacciatore is to die for."

Through the window, I see a scattering of tables. Each is covered with a checked tablecloth, a cheery vase at their center. Archback chairs in various states of repair circle each table, a few holding diners. Two kids slurp their spaghetti while their parents look on, laughing, and a couple shares a bottle of wine and a plate of scampi. A busser clears a table, tucking cloth napkins under his arm. Joaquin presses on the door and I hear a chime from within.

There's a shimmer in the air as we cross the threshold. Inside is a very different picture.

An expansive dining room spreads out before us. Dozens of tables occupy the space, each with white linen, long-stemmed crystal glasses, and gleaming silverware. Servers in crisp aprons circle the room, attending to diners. The glow of candlelight fills the room. In the corner, a trio of musicians plays a soft backdrop near a statue of Artemis. A fountain below her figure burbles water in a gentle cascade. The artist rendered her in a hunter stance—bow drawn, arrow nocked. From the rear of the restaurant comes the incredible aroma of a busy kitchen. The walls are a giant mural of the Italian countryside.

I turn in a small circle, taking it all in. "This place is gorgeous," I say. "How...where? Wow."

"The mural? It's Palermo."

"I love it." I will time to slow. "All of it."

An older man approaches us, his hands out in welcome. "My friend! It is so good to see you." He turns to me. "I see we have a new guest this evening. Please allow me to welcome you to Anzalone's."

"Ronaldo, this is Lotte. She owns the candle shop downtown."

The man takes my hand in both of his and bows over it. "Welcome, dear Lotte. Anzalone's is here to serve you. If there is anything you need, please let me know. If the two of you will follow me."

Ronaldo escorts us to a table near a window. The large pane of glass frames an evening unseen from the side of a highway. Outside—or what appears to be outside—there is a small village dotting a hill, moonlight caressing the rooftops. "What is this place?"

"A favorite." His voice drops and he leans closer. "At Anzalone's, we can...relax."

I raise an eyebrow. Around us, there is the hum of quiet conversation, soft clinks of silverware against plates. What appears to be a classy, upscale restaurant is hidden from the general public, and I want to know why.

He continues, anticipating my questions. "There are protections here. Rules."

I peer closer at the other customers. A man in a business suit skewers a shrimp with his fork while checking the stock market on his phone. In the center of the room, a family wraps around a large, circular table. They watch an older woman in a paper crown blow on a sparking, single lit candle stuck into a piece of tiramisu centered on the table in front of her. A man with slicked-back, salt and pepper hair catches my eye and raises his martini glass to me from his spot at the bar. Anzalone's has the air of a quintessential restaurant, from the food to the customers.

Next to us is another couple, as vanilla as they come. I assume they, too, are on a date. Guy in button-up shirt and dark jeans, the woman in cream-colored slacks and a sleeveless red sweater. The man is tapping away at his phone when the woman reaches to cover the phone with her hand, then smiles up to his face. I'm about to dismiss my curiosity when I see the woman tuck a tail under her seat with her other hand.

Oh.

Joaquin follows my gaze with his, then turns a wry smile my way.

A server brings two glasses of a deep red wine. He sets them in front of us with a quick bow. "Chianti, compliments of Mr. Anzalone. Shall I tell you about the specials tonight?"

"Yes, please," I say, breathless with excitement, and Joaquin nods.

I try to listen, but my nerves aren't interested in the menu. My toes tingle in my boots and a warmth spreads through my chest. I sit on my hands, unable to contain my excitement. *I am on a real, honest-to-gods date. Me.*

I order a mouthful of words that sound like a pasta dish. I forget what I ordered the instant I meet Joaquin's eyes.

"Thanks for coming. You didn't have to, you know."

"You didn't have to take me to dinner."

"I wanted to." He takes a deep breath, then continues. "And in case I don't get another chance, I wanted to do this right."

Our server saves me from mumbling an inadequate reply to what is the best thing ever said to me when he brings a basket of breadsticks that smell of garlic and parmesan. In need of something to occupy my hands, I remove one of the slender snacks and snap off a piece. I reach for my wine and take a couple deep drinks.

"I may be underdressed," I say, eyeing those around me. "I can't think of the last time I've been somewhere this nice."

"Not possible. You would be stunning in anything," he says, his eyes sliding over me. "Everyone with half a pulse in here knows it."

"And those without a pulse?"

"They're jealous," he says, and grins. "I, however, seem to have missed a spot." He lifts a forearm to examine it. A smear of dried blood mars his warm copper skin. "I do have standards for cleanliness when out with a lady. Pardon me, I'll be right back."

He scoots his chair out from the table. A server appears behind him to hold the seat out and then replace it when Joaquin stands to head for the rear of the room.

Anxiety takes hold in his absence. This sojourn into human normalcy won't last forever, and I'm determined to enjoy every moment. I reach for a second breadstick when a shadow falls across the table.

In front of me stands Rowan in a suit and tie. Whether from broad shoulders or collapsed wings, he looms over me, blocking the light. This close, I see his features in new detail. Undeniably handsome, like a painting come to life. Yet off, somehow. Had crow's feet etched the corners of his eyes the last I'd seen him? The grey of his feathers dusts his hair at the temples.

"Evening. Is this seat taken?" Rowan sits before I can reply and chuckles. "I've always wanted to ask that."

I narrow my eyes, glaring at the interruption, then flick a glance toward the rear of the restaurant.

Rowan smirks. "Don't worry; I know where I am. Unlike your beast of a boyfriend, I can behave."

"He's not my boyfriend," I say, in protection. As soon as the words leave my mouth, I wish they were false.

"Makes sense. Your type isn't exactly suited for the whole relationship thing, are you? Join the club," he says, sighing. "Still, it's fun to put on costumes and play at typical humans, is it not?" He snags a breadstick from the basket, breaks off the end, and pops it in his mouth. Chewing with his mouth open, he continues. "What I can't figure out is what you are doing here in this dinky town to begin with."

"What do you want?" I raise my voice beyond our tabletop, willing one of the staff to overhear, for Ronaldo to intervene. "You should leave," I say, meaning more than Anzalone's. "You won't win this."

The smile drops from his face. He tosses the rest of the breadstick on the table and brushes off his hands. "What would you know, *Lotte*? You're middle management, too." He helps himself to Joaquin's wine, a dribble of red marring the sculpture of his jawline. "I figured that much out from the beginning. Your sisters wouldn't hold back. They wouldn't need to." He reaches for Joaquin's discarded napkin and spits chewed breadstick into it. "Yuck. I've yet to get into this whole eating thing."

Over his shoulder, I watch Ronaldo intercept Joaquin near the door to the kitchen. They lean their heads together in close conspiratory conversation. The older man gestures in a wide arc. Joaquin rests the knuckles of one fist against his mouth, concentrating. I will one of them to look my way.

Rowan waves in front of my face. "Hey. Look, I'm willing to forget our little squabbles—like a gentleman."

"I'm not sure that's an option for you."

Rowan wipes his mouth, then drops the napkin on the tablecloth. He takes another gulp of wine, then leans forward. "Come on. Haven't you ever wanted a vacation home? An escape?" He grins and winks at me. "Oh wait, you got one."

I glance around us, but no one appears to notice that my date swapped out for an invader. I hiss under my breath, "I am not *on vacation*. Now get out."

Rowan shakes his head. He pushes back in the chair to set one ankle over the opposite knee. "You know damn well what's here. You've felt it, even if you haven't seen it. Don't tell me that isn't why you're here. You aren't the only one who deserves a fresh start, a break from the burdens of the past."

"Most don't murder innocent people on their so-called vacation."

Rowan brushes off the barb. "That old wizard was far from innocent, and you know it. Same for that bartender. Wouldn't surprise me if they were working together to keep us out." He purses his lips, then takes another swallow of wine. "Anyway, I came here to say you can tell your boyfriend to relax. I don't need the amulet. Our search paid off."

I ignore his accusation. "You found the bus station and bought a ticket?"

Rowan scoffs. "Better. Something more—efficient."

"A jet?" My pulse races, and I twiddle my thumbs, one over the other in a blur of movement. What have we missed?

Rowan swirls the wine glass on the tablecloth. A splash of liquids spatters onto the white linen. The red stain spreads through the fibers.

"It's merely a problem of acquisition. Age-old issue. Someone finds a treasure. Stumbles across something that can change the course of a life. Then what would they do? Never share it or make it known. No, they keep it hidden, layered in wards, keeping others from a new life. With-holding freedom. You're so-called innocent was one of those."

"Taking something that isn't yours—or anyone else's—

has started wars since the dawn of time. How is your behavior any different?"

"Running away has been how cowards avoid their destiny since the dawn of time. How are you any different?"

His words sink straight into my heart. It is as though the restaurant statue comes to life, the aim of Artemis true and unrelenting.

"This may surprise you," he adds, softer now, "but I plan to share. For a fee, of course. If I'm going to make a go of this... world." He waves his hand in the air.

A server spots his hand and starts our way. With a brief shake of my head, the man backs off. I need more information.

Under the table, I grip my fork and squeeze. "Your one and only grand plan this whole time is to become a glorified *weirman*?"

His face jerks as though I slapped him. "And live the life of the chained? Hardly. We plan to have options, the ability to choose the when and where. Not like some discount market greeter." He scoffs and tuts at me, as though I missed part of his ludicrous plan.

"You underestimate those tasked with guardianship."

I've offended Rowan. He pushes back from the table and frowns at me. "You can't be talking about that pathetic half-born who got lost on his way from the second century." A corner of his mouth kicks up. "Or do you mean his lapdog? Aw, honey. You and I both know he's a short-timer."

Behind Rowan, Joaquin and Ronaldo head our way. As they walk, Joaquin makes a frame with his hands and holds it to the walls. Ronaldo nods, taking notes on a small tablet.

Anger takes hold of me now, my nerves steeling. I'm on a date, my first—and possibly, only—and I'm missing it. I give Rowan an icy stare. "Why are you telling me this? You know the minute you get up—and you *will* leave—I'll tell Joaquin what you said, and he and Ansel will put an end to this stupidity."

The amused expression drops from Rowan's face. His eyes are navy, with flickers of light. I regard the creature before me, lithe and powerful, who's had nothing but time to rot in resentment of a power held just out of his reach. He presses his lips together and drums his fingers on the tabletop as though dealing with a petulant child. He spreads his hands apart, palms up. "I'm giving you an opportunity." All humor leaves his voice. "You can't be blamed for wanting to play with toys. Gods know you must've gone a bit mad here with so few of our caliber for company. Stop wasting time with small fish."

"I've been fine," I say, teeth gritted. We both hear the lie.

"Join us. This," he says, "is phase one. A trial. You have the chance to reign with us. Be there from the beginning."

I shake my head. "This is madness."

He leans over the table and whispers, "I know who you are, Lotte. You would be *worshiped*. Let me put you on the pedestal where you belong."

His words stun me. My thoughts swim in a complicated whirlwind of loneliness and kin, power and community, fate and claim. I hate myself for considering, but to claim I ignore the weight of his offer would be against my nature.

As I open my mouth, unsure of what will come out, a whirlwind of feathers and fur catapults out the door. I get up from my seat and rush out behind.

Outside, breathless in the night air, I parcel out the two bodies wrestling in front of me. A great, winged beast grapples with a massive black canine.

Wolf-like jaws clamp onto Rowan's neck. The two tumble across the strip, kicking up dirt. The animal is strong, its paws landing forceful blows, but Rowan holds his own, maneuvering what is left of his wings to block.

A semi truck barrels its way down the asphalt, honking. Brakes squeal. Unable to pry the jaws off his neck, Rowan forms a fireball between his palms and smashes it against his attacker, who yelps. Rowan tosses the beast under the approaching wheels and launches himself into the sky.

CHAPTER
SIXTEEN
JOAQUIN

Every inch of my body burns. My skin retired to the tropics and left my flesh to collect road grit.

I moan, nerve endings screaming. I identify the surface below me as blacktop. My feet ignore all commands to stand, let alone move. Fingers on my right hand twitch as my heartbeat thunders in my head.

"Don't move," an angel whispers from above.

An owl hoots from a telephone pole, and the night air caresses every inch of skin not covered by fabric. The pain screams through my nerve endings, and I open my eyes to find her face near mine.

The glow from the moon creates a halo behind her raven locks that brush my cheeks. I shift and wince, and what appears to be a restaurant tablecloth slides from my shoulder. I smile through the pain. "Am I dead?"

"You've given new meaning to the term roadkill," she says. Her eyes scan my body, and she bites her lip. "But dead? No. Now quit talking before you make it worse. The nurse is on her way."

Worry, and something like longing, deepens her frown. The owl hoots again, its dark shape blotting out the stars in its silent flight above. Before I can ask what she sees, her lips brush mine, and everything goes dark.

"I'm going to pluck each rotten feather from his wings one by one and cram them down his throat until he chokes to death on his own bullshit."

"I'll make the popcorn," I manage to croak.

Ansel glares at me. "Godsdamn you. What have I said about plan first, fight second?"

My lips crack as I run my tongue over their dry surface. "That you're better at it?"

The corner of Ansel's mouth twitches. "You'll be the death of me, friend."

"We both know that's not how this fairytale ends." My limbs are dead weights, so I attempt to move my neck. Pain shoots through my spine like wildfire.

"Easy there. Far too many close calls in a row." The nurse leans over me. She smells of roses, and diamond studs wink at her ears. From what I can see in my immobile position, she wears a navy satin sheath.

"New nursing uniform? Seems impractical, but if it works for you…"

Calls for another round and the clatter of dishes below interrupt my teasing. Memories from the evening fight for airtime among my thoughts.

"You weren't the only one who was on a date tonight." She winks at me as she probes my guts with a soft touch.

"Who is the lucky guy—girl?

"Make it through the night and you can buy me a beer. We'll trade stories." She sets her hand on one of mine. Warmth seeps in. "Meanwhile, take it easy—okay?"

I nod as I exhale, a slow resignation. "You know that's not in my skill set."

She snaps her bag closed and scrutinizes me. "And how's that been working out for you?"

I picture my angel, her violet eyes. Then, the face of another from long ago. I squeeze my eyes shut against the thoughts. "It's not."

The nurse rests a hand on my arm and gives me a light squeeze. The stethoscope slung around her neck is out of place around her bare shoulders. A tendril has escaped her updo, and she tucks it behind her ear. "You aren't interested in my medical advice, so hear me out as a friend. A life with love is worthwhile, no matter how short. No one stands a chance against Time. But when we live fully, every minute of every day, we give that bastard the middle finger, right up until our end."

I don't speak as chills wash over my body. Whether from her healing, her words, or the sinking reality of my options, I'm shattered, laid raw before her.

She shoulders her bag, brushes a lock of hair off my forehead, and heads for the door. I hear her tell Ansel, "Big bill this month."

"He's worth it. Most days."

With a snick, the door closes behind her.

"Pity party over?"

"Think so," I say.

"Good." Ansel is never one to linger on affection.

I try to sit up, but my muscles scream in protest. A headache gives me vertigo, and I wretch over the side of the table. My veins alternate between fire and ice as blood once again pumps through my body, bones re-knitting a framework.

"Where is she?" I swipe at my face with the back of one hand, a clumsy move. More flashes of memory. Her face frozen in abject horror as she sees me crushed in the street. Wrapping her arms around my human form, flesh bare in the night. She closes her eyes and whispers over me as I lay there. Helpless as my life blood drains out onto the pavement. Where her hands clutch at my back, a glowing warmth spreads. Shouts over her shoulder, the screeching of tires. Many hands load me into a car and every pothole is torture.

"She left," Ansel says.

"What?" Again, I attempt to lurch to my feet. Instead, I

manage to topple off my makeshift bed into a pile on the floor. I curse, a helpless bag of meat and bone.

Ansel growls and stoops to lift and then dump me back on his desk. "You'll only make things worse if you move too soon."

I drop my head into my hands. "And your bedside manner could use some work. You said she left. Where did she go?"

"I was hoping you could answer that. Told Ronaldo to call me and the nurse, then split."

I lift my head. "But how? I drove us on my..."

Ansel lifts both eyebrows, waiting for me to catch up.

I groan and press my hands to the side of my face.

"Think," he says. "With what few brain cells you have left after getting plowed into by a thirty ton truck. Where would she have gone?"

I rack my brain across the minutes before I went black. Arriving at the restaurant, taking a seat across from one of the most beautiful women I've ever seen. Getting up to talk to Ronaldo to make a commission. Seeing *him* in my seat. Blind rage firing from all neurons as I stalked back to the table. Overhearing an offer and the confirmation that more of his kind are on their way.

The offer. To Lotte.

I snarl, and Ansel steps back. "Glad to see the beast has rejoined us," he says. "Have a location?"

They offered to revere her, bring her along in their new utopia. Did she run to them—decide she wanted a piece of this new world?

No. She wouldn't have. Couldn't have. *Could she?*

"Get me transport," I growl.

"One step ahead of you," Ansel says. "Iris will lend you her bike—on two conditions."

I flex both wrists before pressing up to my elbows. I push myself up and swing my legs over the edge of the desk. My chest heaves as I pause there. With a slow twist of my spine, I snap my vertebrae back into place. "Shoot."

"First, quit calling her greenhorn. We underestimated her."

I snort. "And second?"

The door to Ansel's office swings open and Iris breezes in. She pulls on a pair of leather gloves, a helmet under one arm. "I'm coming with you."

I sigh. "Let's go."

Outside, I ease one leg over the bike, huffing with effort.

"Keep your hands in the Friend Zone," Iris says over her shoulder, starting the engine. She noses the bike out of the alleyway and onto the street.

"Thank you for this—Iris."

"My pleasure," she shouts to the wind as we pick up speed. "And yes, you will owe me one."

"One what?"

She ignores my question and heads north. Before we left, I drew her a map in Ansel's office. Long row of buildings, just off the highway. The trailhead will be tougher to spot at night, but my senses strengthen by the minute.

We pull off near the shops. Attempting to hide the bike after a roaring engine approaches the area would be futile. If I'm right, distance will mask the noise of the motor.

I test my ability to walk after a shaky dismount. With each step, my muscles swell and stretch. "This way," I say, spotting my bike at the side of the building.

The shops are long dark. A few streamers dance in the night breeze, and a loose travel flier lifts from its pocket outside the door of the agency. Mountains loom ahead, their depths shadowed in what remains of the night.

We move in sync toward the trail. Long ago, I perfected walking without sound, slinking through the dark. I'm pleased I cannot hear Iris's footsteps behind, yet know she follows.

At the trailhead, I pause. "Wait here. Whatever is ahead isn't your fight."

She shakes her head in silent protest. "No way. I see that limp. We have a deal."

I don't need distractions when battling the supernatural. But I can't leave her out here alone. Should've thought of this before I left the bar.

"Fine," I whisper. "But stay close."

Fifty feet down the trailhead, we come to the boulders. Lotte is there, wedged between two of the granite masses. Crouched, she is still in her silent watch.

I follow her gaze to a figure in the desert, shadowed by moonlight.

Rowan stands, wings spread, head tilted back to the sky. His hands are raised at his sides, palms up, as he speaks in a stream of Latin.

We watch as he raises one arm over his head and reaches behind his back. From behind his wings, he draws a sword that glints in the darkness. He continues his incantations, drawing the blade in front of his face. He thrusts the sword upward with a shout.

Two things happen at once. With a downward swing, Rowan slices into the night. At the same moment, a burst of light shoves him backward, sparks in its wake. He lies on the ground, the sword several feet away.

"Lotte!" I call to her, an unchecked warning.

"Get the sword," she shouts, rushing forward.

Iris races past me. I remain frozen, stunned, my brain sluggish and uncomprehending.

In the air is a shimmering split. A growing crack, through which daylight pierces our darkness.

Lotte puts her hands to the gap, sparks flying from her fingertips. She grabs at the sides as her body is sucked toward the hole. "Hurry, I can't hold it much longer."

I scan the ground for the weapon.

"Here!" Iris shouts from somewhere in the dark. She snatches up the sword.

Rowan is standing now and sees her find. He forms a fireball between his hands as he turns to face her.

"Catch," Iris says and throws the weapon to me.

I snag the hilt from the air, its frigid metal singing in my grip.

Hands free, Iris turns her attention to Rowan. She spins her own hands in a whirling motion. A swirling snow globe of ice forms in her palm. With the grace of a star pitcher, she throws the sphere at Rowan. His fire is doused as snow explodes in his face, knocking him back. Icicles sparkle on his feathers like broken glass. Iris marches toward him, launching more ice bombs each time he tries to stand.

Shaken from my stupor, I race to Lotte and hand her the blade. With a guttural shout, she reverses Rowan's stroke, sealing the gash. She turns the tip toward the earth and plants the blade in the sand in a position of subservience. She is murmuring her own string of unrecognizable words, her eyes closed.

"A little help here?" Iris calls. She continues her onslaught, but Rowan recovers. He rolls behind a tree, sets it ablaze, then uses it as a fiery shield. From behind the flaming mass, he launches more fireballs. "You will regret this!"

I hand Lotte a weight from within my pocket. "When you see an opening, take it."

I shift. Fearsome strength and incredible speed carry me forward.

With a quick but silent circle, I approach Rowan from behind. As he last left me in a pile on the roadway, I want to keep any advantage I can get. Fair fights are for those who can afford to lose.

The tang of blood perfumes the air. For once, I bow to Ansel's wisdom and slink the last few paces, unwilling to sacrifice surprise. The closer I inch, the more he stinks of desperation and decay.

A few feet away, I issue a low growl and lunge for those damned wings. With a tearing motion, I rip one off. He shrieks and I dive for the other.

Rowan's inhuman screams reverberate through the desert as he twists and turns, attempting to throw me from his back.

With a satisfying snap, I crunch the base of the second wing in my jaws. With a jerk of my head, it's gone from his back.

Maimed, he drops to the ground, panting. I leap off him to land a dozen feet away. I spit out rotted feathers and face him to steady myself, ready to launch for his throat. I will end this nightmare here and now, if it is the last thing I do.

Rowan lifts his head, his eyes burning red. "This is when you die, *dog*." Instead of forming another fireball, he reaches back to the flaming tree. A spark ignites his entire being. Rowan is fire, embodied. A creature given in to a reckoning.

He takes one step toward me and then another, fire becoming his figure. I shift my stance. My last, best move must be an end for him, even if it is also my own.

Before I can launch myself, Iris runs the sword through Rowan's back, then withdraws its length. He screams as dark liquid gushes in its absence. Lotte jams something into the gaping wound.

The women stumble back as Rowan collapses into dust.

IRIS SUMMONS a new collection of soft snowflakes between her fingers and deposits them over Lotte's hand, cooling the skin licked by flames.

Back in human form, I huddle behind a rock, my tender parts exposed to the night air.

"Did I...Did you just...Did we..." I struggle to finish a sentence.

Lotte scopes out my vulnerable predicament and laughs. "Spit out your question. Then I'll help hunt for your clothes."

"Nah. Let him hitchhike. That would make a better story." Iris chuckles as she balances the sword over one shoulder. Its faint glow lights one side of her face.

"You stole my bike," I say to Lotte, my speech returning, accusatory. "And you..." I spin to face Iris. "You make ice!"

"Found your pants," Iris calls, waving them in the air. She turns to Lotte. "You sure you want him to have them?"

"*I* want them," I say.

"Hand 'em over," Lotte says, biting her lower lip and trying not to laugh. "Otherwise I won't know where to put my hands for the ride back."

CHAPTER

SEVENTEEN

LOTTE

A bove my shop, I tuck my feet under myself and drape my legs with a plush throw blanket. A tall mug of steaming peppermint tea waits on the coffee table. I reach for it and the heavy leather book resting on the table before nestling back into the cushions.

From my sentinel on the couch, I look out over the square. My breath fogs the windowpane. I draw a finger through the condensation.

Breath. Breathing. Life.

I stumbled home from the bar an hour ago, champagne bubbles tickling my stomach. Joaquin, Iris, and I had regaled Ansel with the story of our night and Rowan's demise.

Ansel examined the sword. He promised to lock it in a safe in the bowels of the bar. I'd opened my mouth to question that decision, but Joaquin put a hand on my shoulder. "There's nowhere safer," he said.

It struck me that Ansel, one of the most formidable beings in the room, had stayed behind during the fray. Why not come with us? A question for another day.

Joaquin tilted back in his chair, hand on the table to steady himself. "My favorite part was Lotte annihilating Rowan via a rusty horseshoe to the gut."

"It was your idea," I said, laughing.

"And Greenhorn here—" At her glare, Joaquin corrects himself, "I mean Ice Slayer, our new swordswoman, is in the middle of explaining how she plans to update your summer cocktail menu. Better get the patio furniture back out."

Ansel frowns, his gaze distant.

"Boss?" Joaquin waved a hand in front of his friend's face to no avail. "Come on, Ansel, bad news or good news?"

"Bad," he says, more command than response.

"OK. More beings like the ones we just dispatched are on the way. They can travel outside of weir locations—maybe. Sounds like they want to build a community of some kind."

"Not happening. I've got days left."

"But now, for the good news. You have the fancy sword they used to get here. That's got to slow them down. Buy us time. And now that everyone's...abilities...are on the table, we'll come up with something."

Ansel worked his jaw. We waited, patient, not daring to speak. There was something he had to say. His eyes, a sky of possibility, ranged from the palest gray blue to a deepening cobalt. They settled on cerulean as he shook his head. "I can't get in. I've tried everything."

Joaquin shrugged. "Maybe that means nobody can get in. I'll put that in the positive column."

Ansel shook his head and stood up, taking his drink with him. "I won't be good company tonight," he said. "You all enjoy yourselves, on me." Turning the sword in his hands, he moved off to the back stairs, lost in thought.

"Guess I better get back to the other customers," Iris said. She turned to me. "We still on for brunch tomorrow?"

I didn't hold back my wide grin. In the same week, I'd have my first date and my first girls' brunch. "I'll see you at ten."

Iris returned the smile, looked to Joaquin, then back to me, and winked. I blushed and turned my head to hide my cheeks.

"I should get home," I said to Joaquin.

"Would you like company? I could walk you. These shaky

legs should make it at least that far." There was a twitch at his jaw, as if in surprise at his own words.

"I'm told you need to rest. Nurse's orders."

"What does she know? "

"You rest up," I said, breezing past his question. I stood up from the chair. "See you soon?" That promise lay between us on the table, alongside the soft rejection.

He nodded, gave me a tight smile, then headed for the bar stools.

My emotions knotted in my stomach the entire walk home.

Back in my apartment, sequestered from all that happened and that came before, I am no less uncertain of my feelings. Some fires burn hot and fast, while others smolder regardless. The risk of destruction remains the same.

I turn my attention to the book open in my lap. I spread my hands across an aged photograph occupying the bulk of the page. My sisters smile back up at me, their fairest masks on full display. CC with her shining eyes and sharp wit, and Triss, ever serious. We'd explored a mountainside that day, gathering dandelions and braiding crowns. My sisters were all joy and laughter back then. I miss them.

With a careful hand, I lift the page to view the next memory. A familiar photo tumbles out and falls face down on the floor.

At a glance, I know what it is, know who I will see when I pick it up.

The paper is soft between my fingertips, worn from constant touch. I flip it over, and my breath catches in my throat. Will it always hurt like this, the assault of memory?

A tear snakes its way down my cheek and falls onto the picture. I brush it away with my thumb and clutch the image to my chest.

The last time I'd let someone in, the last time I'd allowed myself to linger along someone's skin, tracing their fine lines, freckles, and musculature, I paid dearly for my mistake.

That couldn't happen again. Not to me. Not to anyone else.

I need to stifle the flame before it burns any further. Before *I* burn anyone else.

I allow myself another moment to linger over the image before tucking it deep within the pages and closing the book with finality.

Godsdamn temptation, this will be hard.

EIGHTEEN

JOAQUIN

In the atrium, I pause beneath the tree. Its gray branches stretch and twist upward, leaf buds taking shape at the tips. Spring is on the horizon, however distant. I walk its perimeter, yet see no suggestion of the silver threads from before. I rest a palm against its trunk. The wood is smooth and cold beneath my palm. In reflex, I pat the surface as if to assure us both.

The interior of Morgan's is dark and quiet, not unusual for a Sunday morning. Ansel stands behind the bar, shoveling food into his mouth while he pages through the newspaper.

I mount the stool across from him, a slower process this morning. "Any chance there's extras?"

Without looking up, he reaches behind the bar and pulls out a plate covered in tinfoil.

"Bless the stars," I say, peeking beneath the foil covering, "you are the man of my dreams." He lifts one eyebrow without looking away from the paper and I reach for a fork. "What? You're a fabulous cook. A guy could do a lot worse for a best friend."

Ansel grunts in reply and reaches for the coffee carafe behind him. He refills his own mug before filling a second for me. The aroma of roasted beans fills my nostrils and I dig in, starved. Biscuits, eggs, potatoes, sausage, and some kind of mushroom hash make for a picturesque meal.

"Outstanding," I say, wrapping my second biscuit in a paper napkin for later. "Rosemary, thyme, chili powder, and a hint of..." I give him a mock frown as though considering. "Ah yes, bitterness. What happened?"

My boss is one of those people who cook when they're irritated. He calls it a meditative process, says it allows him to work through his frustration. Seems a healthy enough coping strategy, especially when it means I get a homecooked meal.

Ansel swallows his bite. He spears a clump of scrambled eggs and watches them jiggle on the end of his fork. Using his tongue to clean his teeth, he says, "Lawyer called. They rejected my bid. Some long-lost relative from Chicago wants to keep the place. Make a go of it," Ansel says, his words dripping with distaste. "Just what we need, another midwesterner who finds the place charming, the weather mild, and who loves the idea of selling cheap kitsch to tourists." He jams the egg bite in his mouth and chews.

"Hollis had a family?" The shop owner had kept to himself. Customers came and went of course but never the regulars that signal a family, a lover, or any regular presence. I'd considered Hollis a recluse. Inconvenient for my and Ansel's purposes, but a harmless loner. "That's news to me."

"I can't even get inside the place, let alone do my job. What if Rowan was telling the truth? That old codger may have been batshit, but he was a useful ally of sorts."

The lightbulb above the bar crackles on, and a breeze swings the door to the kitchen as the temperature tumbles.

I draw my jacket tighter around my chest and zip it up. "Let's not jump to conclusions. You could talk to the new owner, one on one. Explain things. You might convince them to sell." Ansel growls, a rumble that rattles the glasses behind him. I rescue my coffee cup from tittering off the edge of the bar. "Then again, maybe take me with you. I'm told I'm charming."

"Six years, three hundred forty-five days, and seven hours," he says, his face darkening.

"You'll make it," I assure. "There's time. It's not like someone will up and move to Prescott tomorrow. They probably live in some high-rise in the finance district. It'll take weeks—no, months—for them to get here. You'll be a free man by then."

Ansel, aware of the storm brewing within his bar, fills his lungs then exhales through his nose. Gritting his teeth, he says, "That's easy for the unchained to say."

His words sting, but he speaks the truth. I can't know what it's like to be bound to one place, a slave to a cause you didn't choose.

"We'll do whatever it takes, I promise."

He sighs and pushes himself back from the bar, grabbing my plate and his own. "With my luck, I'll be chained to this netherhole forever."

"Don't for one minute pretend there isn't a part of this place you love and will miss. Like Sunday breakfasts with me."

Ansel grunts. "You're no good to me if you keep getting your ass kicked."

I laugh and salute. "I'll do my best to behave."

"Will not."

On my way out the door, I flip the sign to open. I've got a full day ahead of me and I'm ready for it. Lotte has yet to respond to any of my messages, but I'm not worried.

"Do me a favor," Ansel calls to my back.

"Yes, boss?"

"If you see anything unusual today, call me."

I nod, solemn, and slip out onto the sidewalk.

In front of the shop, the street is bustling. The early crowd ducks into art galleries and wine shops, loops scarves around their necks, and call to each other in greeting.

From the street corner, I see the lights on in the candle shop. I look down at my phone again. Nothing. Maybe she's slammed with customers. Or she left her phone upstairs. No matter, I'm a patient man.

I shrug and shove my phone in my pocket as a moving truck rumbles down Montezuma. When the vehicle pauses in front of Hollis's shop, I dash back down the street, slip into the alley, and climb the fire escape. From my rooftop view, I peer down at the new commotion. One mover is outside the truck gesturing for the other to reverse.

Once parked, the passenger rolls up the back door. The driver consults a delivery manifest before addressing the combination lock on the front door. With a few button presses, he's inside and they begin to unload. Boxes upon boxes, several lamps, and one of those fancy couches missing a back on one end are carried through the door.

I sniff at the air, but there is nothing unusual about the men. Two people who work up an honest sweat for a living, one who lives with an old lady who smokes and the other has a passel of kids.

The one with the kids picks up a box to scrutinize the labeling. "There are red label boxes, red and white striped labeled boxes, and boxes with blue labels, some of which have the writing highlighted and some do not. I can't make sense of any of this. Powder room, huh? Has she ever seen this place?"

The other mover picks up the manifest and flips back through the pages. "I'm running out of room in the kitchen. Where does she want us to put all this extra stuff?" He tosses the useless packet on top of a stack of boxes and hoists the load into his arms. "We've got another job this afternoon. If she can't be bothered to show up and translate this fifteen-page set of directions, then I won't get too worried if a few boxes are out of place."

She? Interesting.

"Works for me," says the other mover. He stacks a few boxes before lifting them in a practiced squat.

His partner scratches his head, then shrugs "She'll have to sort it out tomorrow. You and I will be long gone."

I shake my head, shifting my jaw. "Boss won't like this," I say to the pigeons gathered with me at the roof's edge.

They coo in unison, a hesitant request. I crumble a chunk

of the heavenly biscuit into a delectable, golden pile before them. One pigeon, the biggest, ventures close. He watches me in that cockeyed way before diving for the offering. The rest of the flock join in as I brush my hands off on my jeans.

"Enjoy, my feathered friends. I'm off to find some good news."

~

THANK YOU!

THANKS FOR READING! If you enjoyed this prequel novella, please consider leaving me a review and I'll love you forever! Reviews help me find my readers and I am grateful for every one of you.

If there was something that tugged at your mind as you read, please email me at erinlarkmaples@gmail.com. I love hearing from you!

A Circle of Stars, is the first full-length novel in the *Four Crowns* series. Turn the page for a sneak preview...

A CIRCLE OF STARS

FOUR CROWNS BOOK ONE

Snow down my sweater was the worst of it—or so I'd thought.

When I stumbled out of the cab, dragging two awkward suitcases behind, I'd tripped on the curb, bumped into the street sign, then struggled to regain my footing in time for the awning to deposit a sheet of icy powder down my front.

I shrieked, releasing one of the suitcase handles. No longer anchored, the pink behemoth toppled forward in an unceremonious thud.

A passerby, a man with a dark mop of hair and playful eyes, quick-stepped around the boulder to avoid a suitcase handle to the shin. He stopped to help me, levering the bag upright and then leaning it against the wall near the dark green door with brass trimmings. A *Closed* sign hung in the small window, its blinds pulled shut from within.

"There are easier ways to take a body out," he said with a cheeky grin.

"I'll remember that," I said as I fluffed my top to dislodge the snow, "For the next time I attack someone with a suitcase."

He watched me fumble in my purse for my new keys before reaching to take my other bag. "Allow me. Pure self preservation."

"Are you the neighborhood welcoming committee?" I

extracted a door key attacked to a ring with a plastic fob printed with *Apothecary*.

He tipped his head to one side and smiled. "Depends on who's asking." He maneuvered the second suitcase to lean on the first then squatted to shift a stack of boxes from in front of the door. "This all you have?"

In horror, I realized they were my boxes. A full stack of my carefully labeled, precious to me, boxes. "Those *bastards*."

The man straightened, then frowned. His black eyebrows met at the bridge of his nose. The reflex was instant, targeted. Had he been a dog, hackles would have raised. "Who?"

"Those lazy, cheap, ungrateful—ugh! I left them strict instructions. That's the last time I take a recommendation from thousands of miles away."

"So they *are* yours?" He'd lifted one and examined its purple label.

I took a deep breath and exhaled the air through my nose. Before I left Arizona, my acupuncturist challenged me to reconnect with my breathing whenever I'm stressed. I get a lot of oxygen now.

"They are mine," I said, resigned to my fate. "*My* moving boxes. *My* idiot movers who left my stuff out where anyone could grab them."

"Then we best get them inside, yes?" He tucked the box marked *Sheets* under one arm and reached for another box.

Behind him a pair of crows settled on a tree branch and the street lights flickered on. Night had settled in the town plaza like a blanket. Snowflakes filtered through the air to land on my suitcases, his jacket, and atop the cars. I sighed.

"Thank you," I said. Bone-weary, I jostled the key into the old lock, unlatched the door, and pushed my way inside.

Fecund, damp air walloped my senses like a freight train to the lungs. Steam billowed outward as the warm air within met the dropping temperature without. I wrestled the suitcases inside and flipped on the lights.

"Where should I put these?"

I couldn't reply. All I could do was stare, dumbstruck, at the jungle wall in front of me.

Across countertops, up a bookcase, and around a spiral staircase wrapped a cacophony of vines. The front window wasn't shaded—leaves made for its curtain. Every surface in the place was covered in greenery and potted plants. Giant, holey leaves, long leaves with frayed edges and everything in between fought for space in the shop.

Among the furniture, tables, cabinets, and a makeshift desk, boxes crowded the remaining space. Many leaned in a precarious formation. One had toppled off its stack, spilling silverware over the floor. Shards of blue ceramic and a scattering of dark soil littered another area along with the plant dislodged in the fall.

When I didn't answer, he made a suggestion. "How about by the stairs? I'll get the others." He set the boxes in front of a black, wrought iron staircase that spiraled upward toward the second floor.

I turned a tight circle, taking in the shop. For it was a shop, prime real estate on Whiskey Row, but it was far from what I'd pictured when the lawyer gave me a call. Had my mother seen me, mouth agape, she would have told me to close my mouth lest the fae catch my tongue.

I stared at my surroundings, unable to make sense of my new reality. Pain shot through my fingers upon my involuntary clench of the keys in my hand.

"That's the last of them," my helper said. "I'll leave you to it."

"Excuse me—" I had so many questions, yet only one would surface. "What is this shop?"

"Hollis didn't tell you?" He gave me a wry grin. "Would have thought that would have been on the paperwork."

"It just said 'Apothecary'. I thought it was fancy lotions and soap. Overpriced towels. Belgium chocolate. I thought Hollis imported goods. I had no idea he...But this..." I waved my hand at the vines, the spilled soil, the general spread. "This is...chaos."

The man frowned then, peering at me. "How well did you know Hollis Kohl?"

"He was...my uncle." The man's question nagged at me, probing. "We visited...he visited...I never knew—"

His face grew serious. "Hollis was a good man," he said. Then with a quick nod, he headed for the exit.

"Wait!" My helper was halfway out the door. He faced me again, strain in the lines at the corner of his eyes. "You didn't tell me your name."

He flashed me a sincere grin. "Joaquin." He nudged his chin toward the brick wall, covered in green. "I work next door."

Before I could pepper him with more questions, he disappeared into the swirl of snowflakes.

Enjoyed the preview? You'll love A Circle of Stars, *the first full-length novel in the* Four Crowns *series. To stay in touch about all book updates, subscribe to my newsletter at erinlark.com*

READ THE SERIAL

Love the Four Crowns crew? Read the companion serial, *Weir Walker*—as I write it—for free on Ream! Follow me and other authors you love for access to exclusive benefits for our super fans.

Hope to see you there!

ACKNOWLEDGMENTS

A big thank you to Kathy, Shelagh, and Jamie for the many tours of Prescott and the valley, not to mention the countless nights of good company, food, and storytelling. Whether for brunch or late into the night, Whiskey Row is nothing without you.

My appreciation to the tireless Terrilani Chong for her enthusiastic willingness to jump into a new series and genre from an ocean away.

Thank you Paula Lester for the editorial services and your early Joaquin fandom.

Three cheers for Tara, Stephanie, and Mariah, my round two readers.

Love to Bryan for calling me a beast (as a compliment!) and serving as inspiration for every love interest I write.

...and to Ava. Thanks for being my number one cheerleader, even if "kissing books" aren't your jam.

About the Author

Erin is a lover of fountain pens and the trail they leave behind. She is the award-winning author of the *Four Crowns* romantic contemporary fantasy series and the companion web serial, *Weir Walker*. Her work is highly praised for its heart and snark as well as her knack for breathing magic into the everyday.

Erin is a diehard gadabout, champagne fanatic, collector of houseplants, and firm believer in the tender and wild. A native Arizonan, when not behind a keyboard, you'll find her under the stars, howling at the moon.

ALSO BY ERIN LARK MAPLES

Four Crowns Series

Weir Walker (On-going Serial)

Fallen (Prequel Novella)

A Circle of Stars (Book One, Summer 2024)

Tiara Borealis (Book Two, Fall 2024)

www.ingramcontent.com/pod-product-compliance
Lightning Source LLC
Chambersburg PA
CBHW030313130626
46549CB00002B/840